Catherine Howard is a new author who has produced her first book: *John George's Island and the Vamcreeper's Curse*. She has been inspired to write this first manuscript in a series of three by her love and interest in nature and the natural world. Observing her own children's energy and enthusiasm has also helped her with many ideas to create a fun-loving adventure theme which is detailed throughout the story.

Catherine Howard is originally from Manchester in the United Kingdom but currently lives in Lucca, Italy, with her husband, two children and three pet dogs.

I would like to dedicate this story to my beloved father, Mr Raymond Howard, who is certainly a big inspiration in my life. I would also like to dedicate the book to my two precious children, Valentina and Federico, who have given me so many ideas in creating this series, and to my wonderful mother, Mrs Barbara Howard, who from day one has always supported me. With love to you all.

Catherine Marie Howard

John George's Island and the Vamcreeper's Curse

Austin Macauley Publishers™
London • Cambridge • New York • Sharjah

A CIP catalogue record for this title is available from the British Library.

ISBN 9781788239127 (Paperback)
ISBN 9781788239134 (Hardback)
ISBN 9781528953931 (ePub e-book)

www.austinmacauley.com

First Published (2019)
Austin Macauley Publishers Ltd
25 Canada Square
Canary Wharf
London
E14 5LQ

My family and friends, who have been a tremendous support line and a source of inspiration in respect of creating this book. A big warm thank you goes out to my wonderful nephews, Zak and Nathaniel, who along with my own dearest children, Valentina and Federico, have never stopped encouraging me to write this adventure series.

Part 1

Chapter 1

The Metropolis, 2050

One morning, way, way in the future, John George awoke with a notion. It had been his dream for many years to discover the 'Magical Island' nestled in the crystal blue waters. This dream had been inspired ever since he found the secret map tucked away inside an ancient manuscript which he had discovered in the Natural History Department in the City Library. It had always been and sure was a Big!!! Big!!!!! Secret and he had kept it to this day.

John George looked lovingly towards his two faithful friends. Jericho, the husky dog; and Lizzy, the most adorable white canary. The three of them were inseparable and always knew what the other was thinking His friends had always known that one day they would set sail in John George's Boat, which would eventually become a life-changing experience. This journey was to be a discovery of a lifetime, not only for the intrepid three but for the rest of mankind and the good of the planet.

The vessel which was to take them was a striking blue and white sailing boat that John George and his father had worked on with much care and attention.

They had lovingly restored it from an old shipwrecked relic. It had washed ashore on the banks of the City Port.

'Shipwreck Ahoy'

"Dad, let's go out on our bikes today, what do you think? I feel an energy rush coming on and something tells me we need to head in the direction of the City Port."

“Hold your horses. That’s fine by me, son. It sounds like a great idea. But first, you know Dad can’t leave the house without his caffeine fix.”

“No worries,” called out Mum, who had just entered the kitchen. “Coffee will be ready in less than five minutes.”

“Wonderful,” Dad perked up and soon the kitchen was awash with the homely aroma of freshly ground coffee.

Suddenly from the direction of the garden, Jericho, the husky bounded in with so much enthusiasm, closely followed by Lizzy, the canary. They were delighted at the prospect of going out with JG and his dad. This usually meant a long or shall we say, a very long adventure. “As soon as breakfast is over, the mission of today will commence. Off to the City Port strikes high on our agenda!” exclaimed JG.

“JG,” called out Mum, “Your breakfast is ready. This will be a good fuel for your bike ride ahead,” commented Mum.

John G hungrily ate his breakfast while Dad sipped leisurely at his coffee. “It is a most beautiful day outside, son. Perfect weather for a bike ride. And, yes, it will be fun down at the Port too. Can we go exploring and identify all the boats in the dock? If we take our rods, we could also do a spot of fishing,” said Dad.

“OK cool!” John G exclaimed.

Bikes, cycling helmets, finishing rods and a pack lunch were quickly organised. Even Jericho had her own special snack, Woofy Biscuits, which were her favourite as she sniffed at the packet in John G’s rucksack. “Not now girl, they are for later. We really need to do some real exercise first. A healthy body encourages a healthy mind,” Dad announced. “So let’s go.”

Meanwhile, down at the City Port, the shipwrecked battered and bashed sailing boat bobbed about at the edge of the shoreline. John G was right in his thinking; a wonderful journey was about to unfold over the next couple of weeks and this very sailing boat was going to play a major part in the big adventure that lay ahead. Some things are just meant to happen.

The busy streets were just coming alive although it was Saturday morning 8.00 a.m. The great sprawling Metropolis had awoken to meet another new day; 21st May 2050.

Now, let me tell you a little bit about the city were John G and his family lived. The City of Hanley was an entire world of concrete and steel. Very modern, fast moving and noisy all

Bright Lights Big City and Huge in both size and population. There was hardly a tree or green space to be seen; this was not a unique problem in majority of the World's cities as they had grown so big that natural green spaces were very few and afar. Most people lived in large city blocks. If they were lucky enough to own a garden, it would be very small. Places of natural beauty such as parks and surrounding countryside were being squashed into the background as a sea of concrete and steel dominated the landscape. The only birds that would fly in the vast murky skies were the black crow like creatures which had built their nests and cared for their young in the concrete jungle.

Life went on. This was the future, but how long could the planet survive and sustain life in this way? Pollution and poisonous gases were a major concern, and John G had a passion and a fire in his heart to heal the planet. He had often visited the library in the centre of Hanley. To John George, this was a magical place steeped in history and wisdom. The building was the oldest in the city, dating back to the early 1800s when the world was a different place. Its high vaulted ceilings and marble floors could definitely tell a story or two. John George felt at home here. This was the very place where he had studied and learnt about the planet and how it used to be when green fields, parklands, trees flowers and a whole host of animals and birds were found in abundance.

Our world told a different story now. John George had a hunch that evil forces had been at work. If you like beings not of this world, in other words, his/her/their goal was to mutate and capture The Planet, conquering Earth, and eventually rebuild their home.

John George, at this present moment, could not explain why he felt this way and could not understand where he had gained this knowledge, he tapped deeply into his subconscious mind but could find no answers.

Anyway, back to the bike ride and the boat discovery.

"Dad! Dad! Wait up. You are miles ahead of me, still life in the old dog," exclaimed John George with a cheeky grin. "Hey now, less of the old business. Your old dad, as you put it, is in good shape and would give you youngsters a run for your money any day."

“Now Dad, don’t get too cocky. I tell you, let’s have a race. We are close to the cycle path that runs directly to the port. Me, you and Jericho. On your marks; let’s race!” and off they went. What a sight. Dad, son and dog racing for their lives. The day was hot and sunny, not a cloud in the sky, but a creepy eeriness. An echoing sound of Metropolis life hummed in the distance. Not a single birdsong could be heard. Only the relentless chorus of the black crow like creatures, circling high above and their beady yellow eyes always on the lookout. John G had always found them menacing. His hunch was growing by the second, with thoughts of a possible connection with the crow like creatures. His out of this world theory was steadily manifesting with each passing day.

Presently the three arrived at the Port. What a place! Now we are talking big boats, skyscraping buildings, busy cranes spouting out convey of steel, brick, glass, and any manner of conceivable building material. Here these evil looking birds had grown fat and furious on the easy pickings of modern day life and grew even more aggressive towards the people with whom they shared their world.

“Shall we lunch now, Dad?” John G asked hungrily. “I am starving. I spotted a bench just facing that incredible looking large, silver yacht.” Jericho suddenly seemed to have understood John G’s interest in food, her ears pricked up and she began wagging her tail. “Why not,” said Dad. “I am rather peckish myself and wouldn’t mind taking a quick sneaky peak at that yacht, you have got to admit. Wow!!!!! She is a beauty!!!!!”

The yacht was breathtaking, strikingly posed with its bullet like structure and sleek silvery lines. JG started to get the funny feeling again that this vessel was not of this world. Although, it resembled a yacht in some ways, JG felt that there was something very suspicious about it as it emulated a strange force like an energy field. It could almost permeate and penetrate your thoughts. You were drawn to it but at the same time you felt like you should pull away fast, and run for your lives.

“I must say JG I have never seen anything quite like this in all of my life. Given the times we have been to the port, this is incredibly unique!” exclaimed Dad, “Just fascinating. I would love to take a look inside.”

"I don't think that would be a good idea, Dad." And at that point, a large black bird settled on the bough of the yacht and stared at JG and his dad with an intense gaze which was almost hypnotic.

"Come on, Dad. Let's move on. I am feeling rather spooked," JG said. On leaving the yacht Dad was still rather curious and enquired a man who was cleaning a rather ordinary looking yacht in comparison. Whether anyone knew anything about this mysterious vessel, the man agreed that he was intrigued as well. She was docked almost 3 months ago but no one at the port had ever seen her owners. The only visitors she ever had were the black birds who often perched on her bough or circled high above.

Um! Very strange. Very strange indeed, thought Dad, JG thought so too. "OK, what shall we do next? Shall we walk down to the shingle beach and grab some rays while the sun still shines?" suggested Dad. "Yes, let's go! Are you up for sun lounging, Jericho?"

"Woof! Woof!" answered the husky as if she understood and was most eager to go along.

The shingle beach was all that remained of the stretch of sand, which was once the end of the port, but greed and lack of concern for the natural planet had cast its sprawling mass, bringing with it the ever-growing steel and concrete which now bore its seed in our world.

"Look!!!!! Dad over there!" exclaimed JG excitedly, "A Shipwreck. I do believe I have spotted a Shipwreck. Quick, let's pull her in," as they neared the boat, they could tell she was rather old. She had definitely seen better days but she had a sense of elegance, adventure and wisdom about her. This boat could definitely tell a tale or two about the vast seas and oceans of many days gone by. JG was immediately drawn to her as if this discovery was meant to be, could this be fate?

"Here, JG, take hold of this," as Dad grabbed a rope attached to the front of the boat, "Jericho, come on girl. Come and help, haul her in." After three tugs, they pulled so hard, they all toppled backwards and landed flat on their backs. Jericho snatched her chance to pound on top of JG and landed a big lick on his cheek. "Yuck! Leave me be," JG shouted, rising to his feet. "Calm down, girl!"

"Dad, this boat holds something very significant for me. It is like you and I coming down here today, all makes sense. I was meant to discover this boat, I can feel it."

"Now, JG, calm down. Let's not get all sentimental about this boat, shall we? After all, it is only an old shipwreck, as beautiful as she may have once been. But just look at her now!!!"

"But Dad, please believe me. Can we take her and restore her to her former glory? She once was, perhaps, better. Even with a modern twist."

"Well, I am not sure, son!" Dad exclaimed. "We could be breaking some laws here. If the Port Police found out, we may be in trouble. What if she belongs to someone?"

"Nah!!! Dad. Impossible! I tell you she was meant for me, she is my discovery." JG looked so convinced, so eager that Dad could not resist. Always up for a bit of adventure himself, they got their heads together to devise a plan to take the boat safely back home so that they could start working on her straight away.

No sooner as they started plotting, the skies darkened and one of the mysterious black birds landed on the bench right behind them, his beady eyes at the ready as if detecting something.

"He looks mean, Dad!" exclaimed JG.

"Yes, he is rather close," responded Dad. It started to rain heavily so they quickly hid the boat behind a large boulder and covered her with washed up seaweed. The plan was to return at dusk with Dad's van and take her home.

"Jericho, please, what is the matter?" She started to howl and growl. The bird like creature had edged even closer towards them and Jeri did not like it, "Shoo, shoo, go away!" and with that, the large bird flapped its ebony wings and took off into the grey skies above, cawing loudly as he went.

Soaring on ever higher, the bird creature (who will be properly introduced further on in the story) was fully aware where he was heading. He had an important message to deliver to his evil counterpart.

Residing in the Northern quarter of the city and eagerly awaiting this important message, was Orbotron, JG's future enemy (although he did not know this yet).

This part of the city was also known as the Financial/Technological quarter of the Metropolis, wherever you looked extravagant buildings framed the skies. The most talented Architects from around the world had come together to design these buildings: glass, steel, aluminium, iron, stone, sharp and sleek edges, angular lines, irregular shapes, uniformed shapes. You name it, this quarter had it. Then there in the middle of it all stood the most outstanding building of all, The Silver Oval, or most commonly known throughout the land as The Silver Egg,

This building over the years had been the talking point of many citizens of Hanley and not to mention, visitors to the city too. It appeared in numerous news articles and also on TV, it had even been used and photographed for the cover of the famous Rock Bank known as Galaxy's End and their latest album; Sky Surfers.

But, its inhabitants like the yacht at the port, remained a mystery. The only living souls in the building appeared to be some very dodgy and rather, muscle bound security guards, who wore the most obscure silver uniforms and had the strangest of hairstyles.

Chapter 2

Let's leave our mysterious building for now, children. And go back to our hero JG, who is about to retrieve his beloved vessel, and to commence a journey of a lifetime that will certainly go down in history.

As the day turned to dusk, and the city prepared to take on her evening role. JG and his father prepared the van and set off once again in the direction of the port.

"Dad, I am so thrilled. If I could only tell you how much the restoration of this boat means to me. It means so much more, it will all become clear in the end." His excitement could hardly be contained as they pulled close to where they had hidden the shipwreck.

The evening was closing in fast. And yes, children, you were correct in your thinking; the evil birds had reappeared once again. Circling the skies, all eyes and ears on JG below and his discovery.

Safely back at home with the boat housed in Dad's workshop, JG climbed into bed quite exhausted. Jericho jumped up beside him and they settled down for a long snooze.

A different story unfolded outside as evil contrasted good, peering through the bedroom window. Yes you guessed it, children. A jet-black bird creature having two beady yellow eyes had perched itself on the windowsill. He would stay there as he had been assigned to do so.

As the end of the week approached quickly, the boat was regaining her former glory but I must say with a most modern twist. As it was a two-week Spring break holiday, JG and his father after work, had plenty of time to spend on the boat project. She was beginning to look magnificent.

Dad exclaimed, "JG when she is finished, you know what? I am going to organise a Boat Launching Fest."

"A what?" said JG.

"You heard me," said Dad louder, "a Boat Launching Fest. A party to celebrate our achievements and in honour of our hard work that went into the restoration of our boat and to top it, A Famous Rock Bank, to entertain us all in rip rocking style!!!!!"

"I think you better check first with the boss, Mum," hinted Dad.

"No probs, will do so. Mum will be cool with it. She always lets me throw parties for my friends, and this one will be one to remember. Yehe! Rock the House Down."

"Come on, Jericho, lets clear it with Mum and then we are off to tell the others the good news!!!"

"COOOOOL!!!!! CCCCC Coooool. We are going to have a boat fest." JG was back flipping and somersaulting across the lawn, "Guys, we are going to have some fun!" he yelled.

"Mum agreed, how she could not," he hugged her dearly. Retrieving his BMX out of the garage, he raced off out of the gate with Husky dog swiftly at his heels.

Meanwhile, on not such a light note, a grey cloud had formed over the financial district. Our evil enemy was ready to call a meeting which would take place inside the Silver Oval. Roderick Shotput aka Eddie Eezzie, Head of Security was sporting the weirdest haircut of them. He had been ordered to step up on security control and now he and his men were to be called upon, by the enemy (their boss).

"Dearest citizens of Mutraculon," bellowed the great voice, "our time has come to finish off what we have started, and that is to regain complete control of Plant Earth, the Blue Planet. Centuries have passed and gradually our plan is taking shape. Our mission will soon be complete. The entire planet will become a steel jungle within the next five centuries. Countries will unite under our rule in eternal concrete paradise. Seas and Oceans will be no more. Fields, meadows, mountains, forests, rivers and streams will become a buried legend and cease to exist under our concrete fortress."

"Victory will be mine!!! Mine!!!!! Mine!!!!!"

"Then the day will come when you, my good citizens, will be able to join me for a new life under my most marvellous rule."

The citizens of Planet Mutraculon cheered in unison, "Long live Orbotron! Long live our Leader."

Their voices and Orbotrons echoed throughout the great hall. The sky darkened outside to an inky blackness, a flock of these strange birds which I will introduce to you now as 'Vamcreepers' eerily gathered above the Silver Oval.

Outside a gathering of people looked towards the building in quite horror and unsettled disbelief as the evil voice was projected onto the panic-stricken streets down below.

No sooner as they had appeared, our mysterious beings had disappeared. As yet, it was only Orbotron that resided on our planet. The great plan was to arrange for his people to invade our world. When he and his mutants had everything, just as they needed it to be.

Orbotron retired to his quarters and only the dodgy security guards were left to clean up the show. It had been said by some that these guys had an uncanny likeness to the famous Rock Band, Galaxy's End. But no, no, no, it can't be Galaxy's End. They are real rock heroes. They could not be mixed up in any crooked dealings and forces from beyond, or could they?

Chapter 3

"Hundred guests, JG? Do you really think our garden and Dad's workshop could hold hundred guests? Are you serious?"

"Well, Mum, you always knew I was a popular guy."

"You are certainly that JG, but really, 100 guests?"

As always JG got his way in the end. The party was scheduled for two weeks on a Saturday, invitations had been sent. This would give him and Dad enough time to add the finishing touches to the boat and for JG to get hold of a rock band with the help of his mate Ricky the Red, who had a famous cousin, Eddie Eczzie in the Rock business. And not to mention time for his mum to get all the goodies organised, obviously. Come on! What is a party without goodies and refreshments, guys?

Back in Dad's workshop, the sailing boat was looking 'mighty fine' in boat terms. She was known as a Junk Rig on Modern Hulls, care and attention to detail had been practised throughout the whole restoration process and it was paying off. As you may know children, this sailing boat is extremely special and will soon be embarking on a planet saving mission on the High Seas.

With her shiny, navy, blue undercoat, pristine white deck and living quarters fitted with all mod coms. An extremely trendy bedroom suite for JG and probably most importantly of all, three sea blue sailing masts to complete the look. She most certainly was a spectacle before your very eyes.

JG was so proud. He cast his thoughts back to his recent visits to the Old Library in the city, where he had first discovered the map of the enchanted island. He almost felt the urge to set sail at that very moment, but no! The time was not quite right. His intuition told him he must be patient. Some more research first, then the Boat Fest and celebrations and then he can depart.

Early the next morning, a little after dawn, JG awoke with a sudden start. All night he had been dreaming vivid dreams of mysterious lands and dark seas, intermittently, a hypnotic voice had been calling out his name. Whoever it was seemed very powerful indeed and had the ability to connect with JG's subconscious mind. Throughout the dream, vast areas of forests and mountains were being eradicated and being replaced with tall sharp ugly concrete buildings against the backdrop of a grey sky. It was raining but unlike the sweet smiling rain of our planet, this rain was almost acidic and suffocating.

JG knew immediately he must return to the Library. It was time he started some serious research, he had only two weeks left before the great launch as he began to mark the passing days down on his calendar.

"Jericho," he called out to his faithful dog, "will you accompany me to the library? Lizzie we also need your help," as she eagerly fluttered inside the special pouch bag that JG had provided for her to take outside.

It did not take JG and his companions long to reach the library. It was a form of habit now. Before he entered, he stepped back a little to admire the majestic building. It was the only building left of its kind in the whole great city of Hanley and it was said that it was more than 500 years old. It had been carefully preserved throughout the years by its team of dedicated staff. *This building commands respect,* JG thought and even more so, its secrets and treasures bestowed inside its walls.

Once inside, JG quickly seated himself in his favourite place; it was a window seat complete with desk and computer by a large crystal glass bay window, which was draped by luxurious purple velvet curtain from which you could look out onto the sprawling city down below. A parallel universe, a quantum leap in time.

He then made his way towards the huge bookshelf, which was jam packed with ancient manuals. Some of them literally dating back centuries, again, he felt humbled by this experience. He knew exactly what he was looking for and it did not take him long to find it. A beautifully bound book out of the finest leather and bronze covering with the title encrypted: THE LOST ISLAND OF SACRED SOULS.

Retrieving the manual where he had first seen the map of the island, JG on opening the book, noticed a black feather flutter to the ground. *That's funny*, he thought, *this feather looks familiar. And if I am not mistaken, it belongs to a Vamcreeper, and that could only mean only one thing. Evil forces have been prying. I can only feel deep relief that the manual is still here in one piece!* He gasped, as this book was crucial to his mission.

Quickly, but with great attention, JG turned the pages to where the map was displayed in all its glory. It was a real map of a treasure island by all means. And if he was not mistaken, JG had to listen carefully, *but no it couldn't be, yes it was,* he could hear the sea as if it was beckoning to him, enchanting him to follow into the great blue yonder.

What he had to do now was to try and find the exact location of the island. This was certainly not going to be an easy task. Thank goodness for modern miracle: the whiz of his generation, the voice activated, superfast, supercool personal computer. JG scanned the map into his device and instructed the computer to give him a precise location of where in the world the island might be. This requirement took the best part of 30 minutes to obtain a result and, by this time the library had started to come alive with more visitors. JG looked up from his seat and on doing so he noticed that he was being watched from across the room by a tall thin figure. He seemed friendly enough but you cannot be too careful with strangers.

JG kept his cool and did not want to appear nervous in front of the strange man. He needed this info and he needed it fast if he was going to discover this Island. So he confidently continued with his work ever more aware of the stranger's piercing gaze.

The computer had done him proud. It had produced all the information requested before his very eyes. This island was unique and like the library, she was the last of her kind on our planet. There were no reported inhabitants of any human form to reside on her land, although, she held a wealth of plant, aquatic, birds and animal life forms. She was a self-contained, self-sufficient Natural Paradise and Wildlife Reserve. She displayed no signs of pollution or interference from the modern world, she was a real gem.

Clasping his precious research, JG carefully logged out of the computer. He took a good look around for some time as he would not be returning to this place. It kind of saddened him because he had always felt at ease here. He loved the libraries, vintage surroundings and all the knowledge it held within its walls.

When he looked across the room again, the stranger had left as quickly as he had appeared. Back out on the streets, the sky had darkened. Jericho had been waiting for him under a tree; she had held her guard well and was more than eager to greet her friend.

As for the stranger, all will be revealed soon enough.

JG was proud of the information he had gathered and was eager to return home. The manuscript was safely tucked away in his backpack along with the printed papers of the map. All the information he needed was securely stored in his personal computer.

Chapter 4

"OK, guys. Ready to head home now, are we?" Jericho barked back, she knew everything JG was saying. Lizzie, the canary, had accompanied them today as she enjoyed her outings too. She could be most useful in detecting subtle changes in the atmosphere, like now was a good example; JG noticed she was growing restless, had she sensed something? *Like she usually did*, he thought. He was right, Lizzie had sensed Vamcreepers, not one, not two, but a whole flock of these mysterious bird like creatures were close on track and gaining on the group of three.

Now is a good time to introduce you, readers, to these nightmarish, prehistoric looking birds. They have evolved seemingly out of nowhere around some 50 years ago. The first of its species being recorded in the fierce out backs of Northern Australia, as these creatures can withstand extreme weather conditions. They can now be found all over the world. And sadly, as the planet is becoming more polluted and environments are becoming harsh, these hellish birds are thriving, within this new environment of concrete and steel. Jet Black in colour, half-crow half-bat with great night vision, their eyes are either yellow, orange or blood red, and their talon's, oh their talon's, these are shaped like giant hedge cutters and are as sharp as a cut-glass diamond.

Their wingspan covers an expanse of two feet on each wing, giving them a total of a huge four feet. Their deadly cawing sound can be heard from dawn till dusk. Some scientists have suggested that this is a constant form of communication. The flocks seem to dwell within a form of hierarchy with an alpha male and female who are seemingly always in control.

To complete their profile, there are as fast and stealth as a small jet plan. So, there you have it. This is one successful living creature, which has evolved out of earth's destruction.

“Step on it, Jericho,” called out JG, “those creepy birds are gaining in on us fast. We need to get home as soon as possible and no sooner,” as he said this, the largest bird of the flock swooped down and headed straight for JG, cawing loudly as he made his descent.

JG peddled even harder, conscious of the precious manuscript and research that he had strapped securely to his back. His super-duper BMX bike gripped the road; JG and Jericho were now at flat out speed, poor Lizzie hung on for dear life in her pouch. The evil bird was closing in on him with talons outstretched. Eyes blood red, flicking ferociously as he focused on the precious research that JG needed so badly.

The vicious bird swooped in again, even closer this time. Another bird made her descent, outstretched talons, she was ready to rip the tail off of poor old Jericho. She turned around and growled and snarled as the evil bird made her stop in her tracks. She began her attack but Jericho fought bravely The Vamcreeper had pinned her down to the floor. JG had no choice but to stop and go and help his beloved friend. The male bird saw his chance and pounded onto JG’s back, his talon’s clutching deeply into JG’s leather jacket. The brave twosome fought on but the rest of the flock were fast approaching.

JG’s heart was pounding inside his chest as he frantically searched for his precious research. The intense sound of the cawing hell-birds filled the sky. They were everywhere, then suddenly as if by magic, a noble beast, a silver Wolf Dog leapt into the madness, twice the size of Jericho. “Be gone. Leave my friends alone,” he howled, “return to your demon master, with a message to choke on.”

“Tell him there is forever hope for our planet. He has not won the battle yet, far from it. Tell him our troops grow stronger every day. Nature will fight back. And now we have our saviour, the very thing that your master has been searching for since his evil plan was put into place. Although, he does not know it yet, we will overcome all evil and regain our rightful home. Now go, leave us!” he flashed his great white fangs, and all the hairs on his long back stood up in anger. Every muscle in his powerful body rippled under his beautiful silver coat.

The alarmed Vamcreepers took to the skies like a black cape, they rose into the distance. The Wolf Dog proudly turned himself towards his new friends. His great size was the first thing JG noticed about him; he was as big as a lion and probably strong as one too.

"How can we ever thank you, sir?" JG announced.

"What are guardians for?" the Wolf Dog exclaimed. "I think some introductions are in order first. Before all is revealed."

"So, I will introduce myself properly to you."

"My name is Gabriel. Well, you could even call me your Guardian Angel, if you like, just as my name suggests. We have already met earlier today, my friend. Think back to the Library and the mystery stranger in the corner. Let's just say that was me without sounding too shocking. Have you ever heard of the term 'shape shifters'?"

"No, no. I haven't!" JG exclaimed, looking rather confused.

There, there. Don't look too alarmed, my friend. I will explain all in good time. For now, let us get you three back home safely. I know those Vamcreepers of old. We are long-time enemies and they do not give up. Well, let's just say their master does not give up."

"Who is their master?" said JG.

"Good question," said Gabriel, "now this will take some explaining. First let's get your head around shape shifting and then I will answer your second question."

Chapter 5

As Gabriel guided the exhausted threesome back through the city streets, they chatted amongst themselves. Gabriel was a master at gaining trust and JG was already warming to this noble beast.

"By the way, how is the Sailing Boat coming along?"

"How do you know about the boat?" said JG intriguingly.

"They don't call me Gabriel for nothing. Now, do they?"

"Well, I guess not," said JG, "you are obviously one talented Wolf Dog," Gabriel smiled proudly to himself and turned to Jeri.

"My dear girl," he said kindly. "There is definitely a spot of the old Wolf blood line running through your veins."

"Well, of course," Jeri spoke, "you could put it that way. We Huskies are virtually first cousins to the wolf. We are an ancient breed, you know? We were bred for strength and endurance," she continued enchanting Gabriel with her deep blue eyes.

"Those Vamcreeper critters are downright nasty. One of them had me pinned down to the ground. So glad you jumped in when you did Gabriel, I dread to think what the outcome would have been if not."

"Don't worry from this point onwards. Let's just say you will have me on board. I have got your backs, as they say in the movies. Hey!" He winked at them all. He had a real humour about him that added more quality to his already charming character.

With all the chatting going on amongst them, time passed quickly and soon enough they were back home safely.

"Well, we got out of that one quick enough," joked Gabriel. JG could already see he would enjoy his new friend's company. The Wolf Dog was just sooooo cool and positive, and a great companion for the imminent journey ahead.

"JG, JG, is that you?" his mum was calling him.

“Quick, Gabriel, hide inside the workshop. I don’t think my mum will be ready to meet you, just yet.”

“OK, no worries, bro. Consider me gone,” and with that, he leapt into the workshop just in time, as Mum flung open the door to greet her son.

“JG, what a crazy morning. Since you have been out, the phone has not stopped ringing. Already 50 people or thereabouts have confirmed that they are coming to the Boat Fest next Saturday.”

“Wow! Mum, great news!!!” said JG

“Wait for it. There is another thing,” Mum continued, “and this is super important, Ricky the Red has found you a Rock Band to perform on the night.”

“Now this is the good bit, you will never guess who.”

“Go on, Mum, don’t keep me in suspense.”

“OK. Guess who? Galaxy’s End.”

“NOOOOOOO!!!!! I can’t believe it’s really Galaxy’s End. That’s unreal, far out! Galaxy’s End will be performing at my Boat Fest. Wicked and wicked again.” JG was off-the-scale delighted.

Mum was SOOOOO proud of her young son. She always knew there was something special and quite particular about him. Yes, he was trendy, yes, he loved Rock Music. He had some cool mates and was popular. But the thing that stood out the most was in a somewhat contrasting way; it was his affinity with nature, and animals, which was growing more apparent every day. His mum, although could not quite believe it herself, had a hunch that JG could actually talk to animals, and that he had a deep understanding for them and, they to him. Call this unbelievable but she was almost positive that this was true.

JG could not keep the smiles off his face. The fact that this famous Rock Band was actually performing at his Boat Fest meant so much to him.

He rushed onto the lawn performing one of his trademark somersaults.

“Mum just off to Ricky’s house so he can give me all the details. One favour – tell Dad on his return from work that this evening we need to give our sea beauty her final coat of paint. Before we know it, Saturday will be here and we will be having expectant guests coming out of our ears.”

Ricky the Red lived on the other side of town, and in order to get there JG had to take the underground.

"I think a little music is in order to get me into that rocking mood. And with what I have been through today, music is sure good for the soul," he told himself. With that he produced his state of the art Bam Fam Dangle portable music centre. These metallic beauties were worth a small fortune, it had the looks and the acoustic quality to die for and every self-respecting cool kid of this generation had one.

The machine was, yes, you guessed it, voice activated, and JG put in a request for none other than his favourite track Soul Seekers Paradise from the new album Sky Surfers by Galaxy's End which had gone straight to number one in the current music polls.

By now, JG had bought his ticket and was awaiting his train. Then out of the corner of his eye, who did he notice looking straight at him? Any ideas, kids? The tall stranger from the library! Yes, you've guessed it. Although, this time instead of being alarmed, JG was cool with it. He knew he was under the watchful wolf eye of his shape shifting guardian, Gabriel.

The Metro pulled in at speed, breaks screeching, all fires blazing, but hey this was normal. Guys, we are talking about the Metropolis of Hanley here. No rest for the wicked. Machines and vehicles don't mess around here, speed and accuracy are paramount for a city of this calibre.

Finding himself a quiet corner JG sat by the window, closely followed by Gabriel, who sat a facing him. It was not rush hour. The train, strangely enough, was almost empty. They had exactly one hour's journey ahead of them. This being the case, Gabriel settled down and seized his chance to explain to our young friend the art and the deep knowledge connected with shape shifting.

"Ha. Hum," clearing his voice, he went on. "Lesson one," he began, "shape shifting or metamorphosis is the ability of an entity to physically transform into another being."

"Wow big words, pretty deep stuff. That's quite a lot to take in," said JG.

"Well, to understand it properly, my mate, I think you have to better experience it first-hand."

"You mean I, I could actually shape shift?"

"Yes, of course. Why ever not? In fact, let us get started straight to it. Meet me tonight in your dreams when the clock strikes precisely 12.00pm. Call out my name three times and I will appear, as if by magic and guide you there."

"Guide me? Where?"

"To the Land That Once Was and the Whispering Planes. You are a very privileged young man, you know. No human to date has ever crossed these boundaries. You will be the first of your kind to enter this magical domain."

"Awesome! Out of this world!" exclaimed JG, "And I meant that literally."

"If only you knew what lies ahead of you, my friend. My task is to help you all I can to share my knowledge of our World and other dimensions in time to enhance your senses to the point where you will actually develop a sixth sense. And this, my friend, is a true gift. One that you must hang onto for dear life."

"This evening a magical place will be revealed before your eyes. We will actually travel there in your dreams but I can assure you the experience will be reality. The dream is only a vessel in which to transport you there. I have arranged for you to meet some wise people. First though, I will be introducing you to a pack of wolves known as the Wild Wise Wolves of the West. Both the wolves and the people will play a most significant part in your quest and without their beliefs and teachings, our battle for Planet Earth would surely be lost."

"Gabriel, what you're trying to say is we will soon be fighting a battle?"

"Yes, I am afraid that is the case."

"Ah well, this is all making sense now. This hunch that I have always had is fast becoming a reality. And the Vamcreepers hold the key to who our actual enemies really are."

"Yes, you have got it kid, you have got it."

"I will tell you another thing, how long have we got left on this journey?"

"Roughly half an hour has already passed."

Chapter 6

"OK, move in closer. We don't want to tell the whole world now, do we?" the train was fast becoming rather populated with city dwellers.

"Now in strictest confidence, recently reports have been filed about a couple of sightings of some strange rat like creatures. At first glance these things appear like your normal everyday rat. But on closer observation the latter part of their body has taken on a mutation in the form of a scorpion."

"Only taking to the streets at dusk, these creatures are becoming a problem. They are adding more pressure to the already fragile ecological system and who knows what effects they will eventually have on the environment. They seem to be breeding at an alarming rate just like our friends the Vams. Soon, we will all fall victim to the mutant curse."

"Let's just call it Evil forces at work again!" JG exclaimed.

"Well, I can tell you I have a pretty good idea who is involved in all of this," said Gabriel with a confident look on his face.

As their conversation terminated, one of these said creatures scurried from underneath his hiding place. Information recorded, where could he possibly be heading with such haste? Yes, you may have guessed it. The same place where the evil Vamcreepers return, the headquarters in the heart of the financial district. The mysterious Silver Oval.

Within his prestigious surroundings, our enemy eagerly awaits this news. An ancient life form dating back to over 500 million years ago, Orbotron from the planet Mutraculon, has conquered many a planet, mutating its life source and geographical/environmental structures. Wherever he travels, he brings about death and destruction as he seeks total control of his chosen host.

The alien, when it comes to creating mutants, is an expert in this field. A great scientist you may say or a madman, as his favourite experiment is to mutate and then create new creatures. This is carried out wherever he seeks control of a planet. And yes, the Vamcreepers and now the Ratscorps thanks to Orbotron have proven to be able to adapt and flourish on earth. These creatures have been mutated to withstand the harshest environments, they have an exceptional ability to colonise vast areas at a rapid rate. Like the Vamcreepers.

The Ratscorps can thrive both above and underground, as their unique respiratory system has been created to cope with both environments. The underground dwellers of the species are much larger, roughly about the size of a Labrador dog. And the underground Vamcreeper has a larger wingspan than his cousins of the skies. The underground Vams are also blind and rely on radar to help them navigate their flights. Though I may say they are equally as vicious, if not more so. Both underground species rarely enter the world above and will only venture into our world occasionally, if so requested by their Master. So, there you have it young readers, just a short introduction to these horrific mutants you will learn more about them at the right time. Now let's continue with the story.

"Well! Well! Well! What took you so long?????" The Masters voice bellowed through the great Atrium within the Silver Oval.

The Ratscorp had finally reached his destination and was ready to present his story to his evil creator.

"Sir, if I may, I have some very important news. Worthy of your full attention, my master." The Ratscorp continued clearing his throat, his long whiskers twitching with anticipation. "There has been a meeting between Gabriel, our shape shifting friend and JG, the gifted young man, with a mission to heal Planet Earth and destroy your plan."

"Destroy my plan? Destroy my plan? Nevvvvvvvvver, who has the courage and the power to challenge me and regain their world? I am the Great Orbotron from our Mother Planet Mutraculon. It will never happen. Mark my words, it will never happen. I have been conquering planets for millions of years. It is just total nonsense that a mere human child could ruin my reign of power just like that."

His booming voice could be heard once again as it resonated outside the oval. Citizens on the streets outside were most surprised and were beginning to become ever more frantic and suspicious of the Silver Oval and its eerie inhabitants.

The team of security guards which looked spookily like the rock members of Galaxy's End were summoned into the great Atrium. Orbotron began, "Men it has been brought to my most majestic notice that this young boy JG or whatever his name is, is due to set sail next week on a planet earth saving mission. As I am sure you are aware, you guys have been asked to perform at his Boat Fest Party, am I correct?"

"Yes, master," the Rock band responded with strange hypnotic voices, "Anything you ask Master, we are here to serve you."

If you are wondering what has happened to these poor unfortunate guys, you would be right in guessing that it is Orbotron who has put them into a hypnotic trance. He has taken partial control of their minds. He does this by the means of tiny implants that he has inserted into their brains which are connected to his vast computer system, which can be found in the vaults of the Silver Oval. More about this later. Let's go back to Orbotron's request and his evil plan.

Chapter 7

“Men, my famous Men, you are none other than the Rock Group Galaxy’s End. You know, I sometimes listen to your music when I am not so busy, you are talented that is why I chose you to carry out my work. I like intelligent life forms especially when I can control them,” he smirked to himself as an evil smile took over his usually expressionless face.

“The Sunday morning after the Boat fest, JG is scheduled to set sail and launch his precious sailing boat into the ocean. He has the map of the Lost Island, nestled in the crystal blue waters. A Natural paradise and earth’s last stronghold and only hope of survival. Thus, destroying my goals of total control.”

“If JG succeeds in finding this island, he could possibly reverse my plan and save Planet Earth. It is chronicled that Flora, some enchanted angel type being, protects this island paradise but she will be no match for my fleet of Vamcreepers and my vicious pack of Ratscorps.”

“Centuries have passed searching for this lost paradise. It exists but there is a protective force around it which keeps intruders away, even my strongest and most advanced computer fails to detect its whereabouts. So, therefore, my only hope of discovery is to follow this young boy; destroy him and the Island Paradise which he seeks. Then Earth will be mine for ever,” he thunders and booms.

“Men, your job is to take my Super Yacht. This sleek yacht has all the power you need to complete the task. She has been docked in the Port for the last three months. And if I care to say so myself, she is a real beauty and is worth a small fortune.” The Great Orbotron does not fail when it comes to precious possessions, “I do have, as they say, great taste. Ahh how can someone be so blessed!” he continued preening himself. This alien was full of self-pride.

“Cool, Man. True Rockers travelling in true rocking style!!!!!” announced Eddie Eezzie, the lead singer of the group. For just a second he had come out of his hypnotic state, Orbotron looked on in concern.

“Hey, Orbotron, my mate,” Eddie Eezzie went on. “What’s in it for us?”

“Well, let us just say for now, give me what I want and we can come to some agreement later,” was Orbotrons answer, “and show some respect young man to the all-powerful Orbotron. You are working for me, remember,” he boomed. He was not happy with the way Eddie Eezzie conducted himself in front of him. He did not like this, he did not like this at all. This hypnotic state was not supposed to switch off and on by itself like this. He left the great Atrium a little concerned, leaving the security guards to ponder over the quest they had just been set.

By now JG’s train journey was drawing to a close. “Next stop, mate. And that will be us,” but Gabriel was already gone. *How does he do that…?* JG thought to himself, *he must teach me that stuff.* JG knew that his guardian had his back at all times, and it felt good. “Hey, my very own bodyguard,” he chuckled to himself. And then as if by magic, Gabriel was before him once again, as JG turned the corner into Ricky the Red’s road.

“I forgot to remind you to meet me in your dreams this evening at 12 pm, call out my name three times,” and then he was gone again. He had changed back into his usual self; the Silver Wolf Dog.

Chapter 8

As JG approached Ricky's house, a wave of excitement leapt over him. Ricky was a great kid and a good friend, JG had known him since primary school and they had always been great mates. Ricky's musical talents were top class, both the electrical and acoustic guitar being his favourite instruments. But, he was good at the violin and the piano also.

As JG reached the front door, he could hear some cool vibes coming out of Ricky's bedroom window. "Ricky mate," he called out at the top of his voice, "come and open up. It's me, JG."

"On my way down, mate," Ricky called back, sounding as excited as JG.

The two friends greeted one another with a cool high five, and a kind of a boy hug, "Come on in, come on in. Saturday, wowwwww! Saturday, wooooo. I repeat Saturday is going to be a realllll blasttttt, big emphasis on the blasttttt. My cousin Eddie and his band have promised to put on an electrifying show. It will be awesome. You see JG; it is not what you know, it's who you know. Hang with me son and you will be sorted. People will be talking about your Fest for months, no correction, for years."

"Sounds all good to me," answered JG, "thanks mate, I owe you one."

"Don't mention it pal. After all, what are friends for?"

"Come up and have a listen to my jamming session. I am working on a new piece. If it's a big hit, you can say you heard it first. Do us a favour though, my mate, grab some snacks and a bottle of coke before you come up. You know where my mum stores them by now?"

"OK, coming up in five."

Ricky's room was right at the top of the house. He had the whole attic space all to himself. He practically lived in a music room, apart from one single bed, a wardrobe and a small couch in the corner. Everywhere you looked there were guitars on the walls, against the walls, hanging from the ceiling on every shelf, and then there was the piano shining right at you, just asking to be played. These young lads had spent many a happy evenings here hanging out together and listening to Ricky play his instruments.

Munching away on their snacks, JG so wanted to confide in his friend about the Vamcreeper attack earlier on and his meeting with the now guardian, the Wolf Dog Gabriel. But what if his friend would think him to be mad, after all, how could a person possibly talk to a Wolf Dog… and then there is the shape shifting stories, the evil forces at work, the map of the Lost Island he found in the library and now the mutant creation sightings. Could all this be in his imagination…?????

“JG, JG, snap out of it. Anybody at home in there?”

“Oh! Soz Ricky, just having a strange moment.”

“Yeh, man, you can say that again. You were in some kind of trance or something, is that Coca Cola going to your head?”

JG quickly piped up and changed the subject, “OK, let me have it,” he went on, “let’s hear your new number, and it better be more than awesome.”

“OK, you asked for it, prepared to be transported to another dimension.” Ricky looked on proudly.

Suddenly the room came alive with an awe-inspiring opening line from the electric guitar, it was so good the hairs on your body literally stood up on end. The rock vibes were electrifying.

“Go, man, go,” cried out JG, loving it, “you better be performing at the Fest with that number. Never mind Galaxy’s End, you are a real star.”

“Not bad, am I? So were you transported then…?”

“Of course!!!!! Up, up and beyond.” JG was impressed. Ricky really did have some talent.

Chapter 9

Back at home, JG found his dad in the workshop.

"What time do you call this, son? You know I have been home two hours and got your message from Mum about the finishing touches and then you turn up when I am nearly finished. That is what I call good timing on your part."

"Soz Dad, you're a real star. She looks the business and more, just how I imagined her to look, impressive stuff, Dad."

"Glad you're happy with the look but enough of the gawking. Throw on those overalls and come help me with the last coat of paint. But before you do that, go and grab me a cool drink. I think I deserve one. And by the way, Mum has had another 50 plus confirmed guests so Saturday is sure going to be a big one!!!!! Are you ready for it?"

"Ready as I will ever be. Ricky is playing and also Galaxy's End, so we are all in for a real treat."

"You mean 'the' Galaxy's End?" said Dad, a little astonished.

"Yes, of course! The real MC Coy," answered JG proudly.

"You certainly have friends in high places," commented Dad.

"Well, you know, I am a pretty special guy," JG winked.

"We had better invite the neighbours or we won't be too popular around here anymore. Hey, JG, do you think I would get away with wearing those tight black leather trousers and getting my hair cut into one of those trendy styles?"

"Why not!!!!! Go for it, Dad. You won't look a day over 18. Everyone will mistake you for one of my mates."

"Cheeky!!!!! Cheeky!!!!! Now go and get me my cold drink."

It was almost dark outside as JG crossed the garden and headed towards the house. He felt like he was being watched, his sixth sense was kicking in already and that is, without lessons from Gabriel. Maybe just being around him had an affect too.

Jericho suddenly came bounding towards him disturbed by the creature that had been watching; some rat like being scurried away into the adjoining garden.

"Creeeeeeeepy!!!!! Spoooooooky!!!!!" JG said out loud, "That thing strangely looks like one of those mutant rat creatures that have been sighted recently. As if we don't have enough with the Vamcreepers invading us now we have mutant rats."

Those guys had worked hard on the foundling vessel, she was complete and fit to take on the oceans and most certainly fitted the profile of a future planet saving sailing boat. Everything that JG could possibly need was there at hand, down to the tiniest detail. His dad had spared no expense, he had even bought and installed a brand new computer system with a state of the art navigation board, voice activated, of course.

JG was so ready to commence his journey but he had forgotten to mention one most important thing; to tell his parents. How could he approach them with this coming event? They had no idea of his intentions, no idea what so ever, and deep down in his heart, without trying, he knew that they would never permit him to set sail alone. He was only 14 years old and just a boy in their eyes.

He would write a letter explaining everything. He simply must go on this journey. This task was set in stone. And on his victorious return, he would put everything right with his parents. Of course, he loved them dearly from the bottom of his heart but this was no time to get all sentimental about things. He had a planet to save, and that very evening he had an important meeting to keep with Gabriel.

Mum and Dad looked quite relaxed as they chatted together outside on the patio, "Goodnight, you two. I am turning in early this evening, I have a few more thoughts about the Boat Fest and would like to discuss the music plan with Ricky."

"OK, love. Don't overdo it. You need your beauty sleep, young man," joked Mum.

"Don't worry, Mum, I will make sure I put on my nourishing face mask, and apply the old cucumber slices to my eyes," he joked back.

Little did his parents know, he would be off to another dimension, with a Wolf Dog named Gabriel and learning the arts of shape shifting in order to save our planet. He soon drifted off into a deep slumber.

He awoke with a start, the moon was shining through his window and the stars had put on a full show that evening. It was a beautiful inviting scene, just the right setting for a midnight adventure.

Glancing at his clock It was still only 11 pm he must go back to sleep in order to dream, he drifted off once again into a deep slumber. Upon opening his eyes, he found himself in his bed but it was not his room. In one corner there was a large pine tree. Then he heard trickling water as if there was a stream close by. The stars and the moon were right above him and he thought he could just hear the howling of wolves in the distance which strangely enough comforted him. Wherever he was, he felt alive and awash with the sounds and calls of nature. He glanced to the side, his clock was there on his bedside table and it was 12 pm precisely. He called out Gabriel three times as instructed and waited.

As promised, the handsome Silver Wolf Dog appeared right in front of him. His deep, expressive amber eyes were fixed on JG's, they were the kind of eyes that could definitely tell a story or two, but gave out such trust and encouragement. JG remained bewitched for a short while as he gathered his thoughts and checked his senses.

"Are you ready?" Gabriel finally spoke.

"You have no idea how ready I am my friend," JG answered in a confident manner.

"Both confidence and enthusiasm are a good mix, just what I like to hear!!!" exclaimed Gabriel.

"I have just one question though," said JG, "please tell me where we are?"

Chapter 10

"Ah, my dear boy, we are in The Land that Once Was, of course. It has been preserved and protected by the Wild Wise Wolves of the West and the Good Tribes People from the Whispering Planes. This is their land and you could say, they are really proud of it. You will soon find out why, my dear boy."

"So, without further ado, let's begin our journey. Come. The Wild Wise Wolves of the West await us in the Mountain Glade. Do not fear them, JG, as they are my ancestors. They will not harm you. Most men have always believed that Wolves are their enemies but this is not so. We fear you as much as you fear us. We only want what is rightfully ours; that is to run free in our wilderness and live as our instincts guide us."

"Although I am only part Wolf, my mother being of Siberian husky origin, my father being a pure bred, very proud Grey Wolf. I have their blood running through my veins. And this, my friend is what you will learn too."

"Cool. You mean I will be learning the nature of the Wolf and there wild ways?"

"Something like that, JG. Come on, we have no time to waste, keep up."

So off into the night they ventured. JG kept a close pace behind his trusted Guardian as they meandered through the undergrowth, each step took them a little higher. This area was heavily populated with thick pine trees and shrubs. At first, JG did not realise they were steadily climbing a mountain of some rather large proportions. The stars and the moon enlightened their path; every so often moonbeams and rays of light poked through the great trees. This effect JG thought to himself was simply magical and to add to the spectacle, hundreds of fireflies danced around, as if to some natural beat.

Those agile fireflies were dancing in time with the wolf cries which could clearly be heard now. Gabriel quickened his pace as his wolf instinct kicked in, he knew he was fast approaching the awaiting pack.

The adrenalin at that moment running through JG's body was second to none, it was electrifying and it could only be compared to listening to his beloved rock music. "WOW!!!!! WOW!!!!! This deserves a double wow!!!!! If only Ricky the Red could be here to live this moment with us." JG was almost flying through that woodland, ever spiralling upwards close on track and keeping good pace with Gabriel.

Suddenly, the pair found themselves in a huge clearing. Gabriel sniffed the air and the ground below, then six gigantic wolves made their appearance; four silver, one white like fresh fallen snow and one jet black. They were magnificent specimens, JG presumed that the sleek black one surely must be the Alpha Wolf, his or her amber eyes were as large and expressive just like Gabriel's. Immediately transfixing and bewitching the pair, such wisdom they spoke.

"Welcome and a big well done!!!!! Upon finding our sacred home," the black wolf began. "My name is Harmony but my tribal name, or shall we say, may earth name is Angpetu, meaning radiant day. May I take this moment to introduce the rest of the pack, ladies first, here to my right we have Snowbird, but her earth name is Angeni, meaning Spirit, this lovely lady is Elsa and her earth name is Aquene meaning Peace. Girls come and meet our new friend," the two wolves gracefully jumped down, from the fallen fern covered log on which the pack were seated in a uniformed row.

Snowbird edged herself closer and in true wolf style greeted first Gabriel and then JG with a lick underneath their chins. All this time, their scent was being registered. Next Elsa stepped forward repeating the action. "Thank you ladies!" Harmony exclaimed. "Now let me introduce you to my males; first up we have, none other than, Gabriel's father, Luke, and he goes by the earth name of Abooksigun meaning Wildcat." There was rather an emotional meeting between Gabriel and Luke. JG could easily see where Gabriel had obtained his gracious looks, and on meeting Luke close up, JG felt almost humbled. Next Tiger stepped forward, a very muscular and athletic looking chap, full of self-confidence and charm, his earth name being Ahiga meaning he fights. Last but not at all least, was Frankie. He was the youngest of the pack, but had such a cheeky look and a real charismatic appeal, his earth name was Ashki meaning sacred child, and he was introduced as Harmony's son.

"So now, young man, you have met the pack. Our collective name is The Wild Wise Wolves of the West and it is our pleasure and honour to welcome you both here this evening, let's wish for a long and trusting friendship."

Harmony continued to address JG, "Young man, you have a lot to learn. Gabriel has told me all about you and I am delighted that we can help you with your most important Quest. So, let us not lose any time. The Good Tribes People await us. We must cross the mountain range you see before us until we reach their home reserve known as The Whispering Planes."

Chapter 11

So, off into the night they went. Harmony took the lead as she graciously picked her way through the undergrowth, following the moon and the many stars that lit up the night and guided them on their way.

JG began to feel the adrenalin rush once more but it grew stronger this time. If only his friends could see him now, he thought to himself, following a pack of wolves and a Wolf Dog out in the wilderness in another dimension, another place and time.

As the pack began to pick up pace and move swifter, JG almost felt like he was flying. His whole body felt weightless, his senses were alive with the calls of nature. *Running with the Wolves, Running with the Wolves* the wind seemed to whisper through the trees as they continued their journey forthwith. The stars seemed ever closer, as close as if you could reach out and just touch them. What a World. JG could only marvel at the beauty all around him. He felt like he had come home.

The pack suddenly pulled up abruptly, literally stopping in their tracks. They had reached what looked like a plateau, another mountain glade right at the top of the summit. "JG," Gabriel called out, "edge in a bit closer my son, catch your breath. Harmony and her pack have a surprise for you. They have something that they would like us to join in with."

"Um, what shall we call it their Midnight Chorus. This is actually an entrance call to gain access into the Whispering Planes. You will be pleased to know that we have nearly reached our destination."

"What did you say Midnight Chorus? Just loving the words!!! Sounds like a cool new rock track, hey now!!! Just let me get a recording of this for Ricky the Red, he could use some natural rhythms for his musical creations."

As JG reached into his pocket searching for and finally retrieving some sleek piece of technology; a musical recording device, and no sooner had he hit the record button, the Wolves Midnight Chorus began, this time led by Elsa. Their howling was soooooo intense but so exhilarating that it touched every bone and cell in JG's body. The true Cry of the Wilderness.

"Come on, JG," called out Tiger. "Don't be shy, join in. Give your vocal chords and lungs a real good work out, feel it from the bottom of your chest. Shove your head back, breath in, look towards the moon, and just let go."

"They say that howling with the wolves is good for the soul, and it should come quite natural to a young healthy chap like yourself," Tiger continued.

"Ye he!!! What a cool trick to perform for your friends back at home!" exclaimed Frankie, with his cheeky grin, "Now let's face it," he went on, "how many humans can say they have mastered the technique of howling in pure Wolf Style? Pretty good trick, if you ask me. For a human, of course!!!"

"You're right. Not many, my friend," said JG.

"I cannot imagine any of my mates ever having experienced anything quite like this!!!!!" commented JG as he waited with baited breath to try out his first howwwwwwwll.

"OK!!! On the count of three, just follow my previous instructions," said Tiger, "and just howl for your life."

"Go for it," the whole pack shouted in unison. "One, two, three and howwlllllll."

JG was trembling from head to foot, but what a howwllllll.

"Wow!!! That must have been 500+ on the rector scale," said Harmony jokingly. "We must be careful; we don't want to disturb the sleeping giant, the ancient volcano, in the region."

"Well, well, my young chappie. I am impressed, that was some howl," exclaimed Tiger, "not bad for a human, not bad at all."

"OK! First lesson over," Harmony approached JG, her amber eyes fixed on his, "you did good my friend, you will learn fast. Quite the natural."

Chapter 12

"Now team, onwards and over. We are close to our destination. The Valley of the Whispering Planes awaits us. We have been granted permission to enter by the Good Tribes People."

"Brace yourself, JG," Gabriel said, "your next lesson is all to be experienced very soon!!!"

"Well, if it feels anything like the last one, I am so looking forward to it." JG was fast becoming addicted to this new natural land, and the freedom and energy it brought with it.

The pack swiftly followed Harmony on her descent down the mountain into the lush valleys below. JG could clearly make out a vast river, and some small circular houses along its banks. *If only I had my camera,* he thought, *the scenery is breathtaking.*

Presently, they had reached the valleys. Harmony eased off into an energetic trot, and the rest of the pack followed suit.

Always attentive and watchful, and in true wolf style, the pack confidently approached the river and finally came to a standstill underneath the protective branches which appeared to be a large Olive Tree. Once again the fireflies reappeared dancing underneath the canopy of the ancient tree providing a natural light source in the black of night.

They quietly waited there; Gabriel positioned himself next to JG as the Wise Wild Wolves of the West looked on. Their eyes searching through the darkness studying every move and sound. They seemed to be embracing their surroundings with every breath they took. From an outsider's point of view looking in on the scene you could agree that these beautiful beings were truly at one with nature and the wilderness.

As all was quiet and as they continued to wait for the Good Tribes People, Gabriel proceeded to chat with JG. He felt that the time had come to explain to his friend how the Wolf Dog Breed had come about, and its connection with JG's quest to heal the planet. As Gabriel continued, JG listened with interest as Gabriel's story unfolded.

Born of Father Wolf and Mother Siberian Husky, Gabriel was, as he had explained, a hybrid animal. For a long time, humanity had always wanted to possess a part of the wilderness. And for generations now, the Wolf Dog Breed had helped them to achieve this to some extent. But, unfortunately, with many complications and some sad tales, some cases had happy endings as man had bonded with their Wolf Dog companion. On the other hand, things had not worked out according to plan. Unfortunately, Gabriel was one of these cases, at six months of age and still just a pup, our loyal friend, young readers, found out the hard way.

Proving to be too much for his human companion, he found himself abandoned. He was thrown out on the cold dark streets in the dead of night, discarded like a piece of rubbish, left to fend for himself.

As this breed was becoming increasingly popular, thanks but no thanks to the Wolf Dog's good looks, they were treated rather like a fashion statement. One night when Gabriel was nine months old, after almost three months alone, whilst scavenging for food, he came across others like him. Wolf Dogs that had joined forces after being left to roam the busy streets of our modern society. As a consequence of this, new packs were formed and these partially wild animals began to take on a stronghold in the urban concrete jungle of our world today.

Gabriel swiftly moved himself up through the ranks just as his wild counterparts would do. He was appointed Alpha Male, leader of all the abandoned Wolf Dogs in the Great Metropolis of Hanley and as his skills developed, he began to have visions. During the night, in his dreams, his Father Luke and a member of the Good Tribes People would accompany him, and would transport and welcome him into the realm of the wilderness, into the Land That Once Was, where he would run free with the wolves, a true pack member, taking every opportunity to learn their ways.

"So now, you know my story, and my connection to this wonderful land," continued Gabriel.

"I am happy to have listened," said JG, "it is an honour and a privilege to have you as a friend. Without your guidance

Gabriel, what I am experiencing now could never have been possible. And I can only learn and gain knowledge from this unique opportunity."

Chapter 13

Suddenly, Harmony rose to her feet noticing that a group of five figures holding lanterns were fast approaching. JG felt both excited, and a little apprehensive as he did not quite know what to expect. Gabriel sensed this and nuzzled JG's arm to reassure him.

"All will be fine, my friend. The Goods Tribes People are happy to meet you. They are so pleased that you have such a deep conscience about the planet. They know you are willing to learn their ways, they are sure to welcome you with open arms." As the group arrived at the entrance to the tree, Harmony sniffed the air and stepped forward to meet them, greeting each person with a customary wolf lick under the chin.

The group then proceeded to settle down under the branches of the ancient tree. No words were spoken as yet; a calm spirit took a hold of the meeting filling the intriguing atmosphere with deep wisdom.

They quietly formed a circular group and beckoned JG and Gabriel to join the circle.

Their lanterns immediately lit up the leafy domain, this is just as JG had expected it to be. He felt humbled, once again, to be in the presence of such beings. He looked above, and through the canopy JG could just make out the moon and stars in the inky black sky. If there ever was a night to learn the art of shape shifting, this would be it. He thought to himself, *This is truly amazing. Cool stuff*!!! He kept on thinking.

The first person to speak was a young man, who went by the name of Aranck – meaning stars.

"JG, we have heard so much about you. Tonight you will, quite literally, have the time of your life. What you are about to learn will become a sacred gift that will remain with you for the rest of all time. You will feel uplifted and enlightened throughout the whole experience but you must pay close attention as this skill will prove to be a most valuable tool for your forthcoming, let's call it, 'Crusade'. When you set sail next week and follow the map which will lead you to the Lost Island of Sacred Souls. By the end of this evening, your quest will become ever more achievable."

Aranck spoke once again, "I have been chosen by my Shamen leader to stand by your side and guide you every step of the way. With respect, Shamen Leader, I think introductions are in order," Aranck turned towards and spoke to a very distinguished-looking gentleman.

"Yes, I agree. Aranck. I will take over from here."

"Hello, young man. My name is Atohi, meaning 'into the woods'. I would like to present you with something, something special. Step forward please, and give me your hands." Atohi produced a precious amulet that sparkled like the mid-day sun, silver and turquoise like the bluest of seas. It certainly was very striking but what made it so precious were the words engraved on the back and they read:

WAN TANKA NICI UN – meaning, may the Great Spirit walk always by your side.

"My Dear Boy, take this necklace. You must keep it close to your chest at all times. And whenever you feel insecure or need a boost of strength and power, this simple piece of jewellery will help you through. Each and every one of my people own one of these amulets. It is crafted from the very river you see before you. As you can see, it is a very special piece indeed. Protect it with your life, and you will reap its rewards."

"Thank you, Atohi. Thank you so much, Sir. I will wear it with pride."

Then a lady who went by the name of Abedabun – meaning Sight of Day, stepped from out of the circle to help JG position the precious Amulet around his neck.

"Thank you," JG said, the young lady blushed as she sat back down, she was about the same age as Aranck, around 16, JG thought.

"Now before we begin our ceremony. Let me just introduce you to the rest of my people who have come to join us on this special evening. We have been expecting you for some time you know, young man."

JG could not help but feel a whoosh of pride sweep through him as he listened to Atohi's calm words.

"Here, beside me, we have Avonaco, meaning Lean Bear, this man is fearless and a great runner. Next to him, we have one of our ladies Aiyana, meaning eternal blossom and forever flowering, then we have our young Abedabun, who helped you with the Amulet, Aranck as you may already know, and if you don't know him yet, it won't take you long," (he smiled to himself) "and then lastly, I sincerely hope not the least, myself. So, there you have it. We would like you to know we are all here for you. Trust your experience with us; this will prove to be one of importance and of course, a valuable asset which you can treasure for all time."

"Now, let us continue with your lesson," and as if by magic Aranck immediately appeared by JG's side. The lanterns were dimmed and the circle moved in closer protected by the wolves and the great Olive tree. Atohi commenced this most sacred ritual.

"Hold hands please. My good people, feel the beauty of nature flowing through your veins." JG closed his eyes and immediately he heard the trickling of water and the whispering wind. They were the same sounds that he had witnessed in the forest with the wolves and Gabriel some few hours ago.

Atohi spoke once more to the circle, "Shape shifting touches the very soul of our people. We are brothers and sisters in nature, and it is quite natural for us to feel as one with the spiritual animal world and our living animal friends."

"My People, let us commence our chant, praise our spirit world and our animal friends," the wise group of people began to chant to a slow harmonious beat, Atohi explained that it was Earth Mother's heartbeat, and asked JG, to join in with Aranck, who had two small drums. JG eagerly took one of brightly decorated drums and proceeded to make music in time with the rest.

"Wow!!! You are pretty good," whispered Aranck.

"Well, you could say back at home, I am a little partial to some Rock music, and one of my friends is a talented musician."

"Sounds great fun," said Aranck, "when I come and visit your world, I promise I will look up you and your musical friends, and you can explain to me what your Rock Music is all about."

"Deal," said JG, and they shook hands on it.

Chapter 14

Atohi moved into the middle of the circle taking Aiyana's hand as they began to dance to the cool rhythmic sounds. "Now we are ready to call upon our guardian animals," the chanting became more intense, and the leafy domain was alive with the sounds of the wilderness.

JG felt, once again almost weightless, his head rather whuzzy but a deep feeling of peace touched him like no other feeling on earth; he felt strong, not just strong but super athletic like he could run a million marathons and still come back for more. Um!!! Extraordinary!!! Why did he feel so alive?

Consequently on opening his eyes, he had been transported away from the Olive tree and found himself within a large clearing, deep in the forest. In the middle of the clearing there was a giant boulder. Again, he heard water. But this time it was louder, rather like the sound of a cascading waterfall.

Where am I? he thought to himself. *Where is Gabriel, the Wolfpack and the Good Tribes People? Surely they could not leave me alone here in this wilderness.* He began to feel rather let down and a slight panic took hold of him.

"Fear not, fear not, JG," the voice whispered through the clearing.

JG glanced upwards and there before him stood a Lion, a magnificent Mountain Lion, proud and bold.

"What, this can't be happening. I must be dreaming, now, I am talking to lions? This night just goes beyond, beyond all reality."

"Who are you?" exclaimed JG. Rather shocked, as probably could be expected!

"Why, it is I, your shape shifting guide, your new best mate, Aranck."

“Aranck, is that really you in there under all that fur and whiskers?” JG could clearly not believe what he was witnessing. Surely this was stuff of movies where anything was possible, no?

“Yes, it is really me but in my Lion form. Come on, don’t look too shocked! Keep up, boy, this is the shape shifting bit we have been banging on about all night. Cool, is it not? We are as one, my lion and I, and now you must discover your animal form. Go, take a look at yourself. Come with me to the lagoon, beyond the clearing and all will be revealed.”

JG could not wait another moment as he sprang into action behind his guide.

Glaring into the lagoon below, JG could not believe the sight before his eyes, he was blown away, “No!!! No!!! It can’t be, it just can’t be. Aranck, is that really me? Tell me, is that Puma staring back through the reflection really me?”

“Well, yes, you better believe it. That Puma you see before your very eyes is you. He is your animal form together as one.”

“This stuff is beyond belief. Awe-inspiring Man, my mates are going to love this!”

“What did I tell you? OK, so you are ready, do you want some action? Would you like to try out your new body? If the answer is yes, see that hill over there beyond the lagoon? Will race you on the count of three, and gooooooooo.”

Off the pair went, Aranck took the lead but JG was close on track. “The others await us below the hill, Atohi must show you something,” said Aranck in his husky lion’s voice.

“Suits you, that voice, deep and masculine!!!”

“Thanks.” Aranck was clearly happy with the comment.

“Go on then, let me hear you roar!!! Please, Aranck roar like a lion.”

“OK, you asked for it,” and with that Aranck pulled up swiftly and stuck out his chest, he let out an almighty roaaarrrrr.

“I must get myself a recording of that,” JG said, “wait until I run it by Ricky the Red. Another way out sound to add to his musical creations, and let’s just say, I quite literally captured this straight from the Lions Mouth.”

“Well, if you are going to make me a Musical Hero, my dear friend, I am definitely going to make it my business to cross into your world in the not too distant future. Maybe try my luck at some of that. What do you call it, Rock Music?”

“Aranck, consider it done. You are welcome to hang out with my friends and me anytime. In fact, why don’t you come to my Boat Fest this Saturday?”

“Boat Fest, what is that?” asked Aranck inquisitively.

But before JG had time to explain Aranck stopped him in his tracks.

“Leave the explanations for later, JG, we have some serious business to attend to now. Atohi and the others are just a couple of minutes away.”

“How can you possibly know that?”

“I am a Mountain Lion remember, I have just picked up their scent, and we are close.”

Sure enough his instincts were correct. At the bottom of the hill, there was a small gathering of animals. JG could make out two Wild Horses, a Large Brown Grizzly Bear, and a Stag with antlers to gasp at. Wow, they were huge!!!!!

Chapter 15

"Greetings. Gentlemen, felines," the stag approached them confidently, and JG knew immediately that this wise soul must be Atohi.

"Well, Well, Well!!!!! JG, your Puma suits you. You carry him well. How do you like the new look?"

"I feel fantastic, it is like I have limitless levels of energy and strength with a big dash of confidence too!!!!!" said JG in a proud honest tone.

"I knew you would like him. But now, you must learn to feel like him, to live like him but all in good time. You are nearly there. Our Aranck here is a good teacher, is he not?"

"Definitely," JG agreed.

"Come forward. My friends," Atohi beckoned to the three remaining animals that were standing guard by the hill. JG could guess that the Bear was Avonaco and the graceful Wild Horses with flowing manes that reached down to the ground were the ladies of the group. They were built for speed and agility and could put any horse to shame on the racetracks back at home, these were JG's thoughts.

"Now we must venture on as the next part of our journey will lead us to the All Telling Lake; her waters hold a secret and she has asked me to reveal this to you, JG. Swiftly now, if you will all kindly follow."

Atohi calmly spoke, "We are to head north. I must warn you, it may feel more than a little chilly as we are heading towards the lands of ice and snow but in our animal forms we will be well protected against the elements and whatever else nature has in mind for us."

The proud band of animals travelled through woods and planes, streams, rivers and mountains, ever heading northwards, but Atohi's words were true. In his animal form, his new Puma look, JG felt no pain, no exhaustion, no fear, just the strong beat of his heart. And from time to time, as they journeyed onwards, he felt sure that the rest of the animal group had synchronised with him; their hearts beating together to the sound of Mother Earth's Drum.

After much travelling, they had finally reached their destination. And yes, it was cold. Freezing, for that matter. In fact, here the sky had changed from an inky black to a dark midnight blue and JG could just make out a fine snow shower. A snowflake touched his nose, the horses whinnied and pawed at the frozen ground and the great Bear stretched out his paws and padded the fine snow.

Aranck quickly took control, and was the first to edge towards the banks of the All Telling Lake. There she lay in all her beauty like a precious gemstone sparkling under the starry night sky.

He gave the all clear in a matter of seconds. Silence fell upon them, apart from the distant howling of the Northern Snow Wolves, "This is a good sound, a good sign," Atohi finally broke the silence, "the Northern pack have sensed our presence and have welcomed us into their land. They will now offer us protection during our time spent here."

By contrast, this was the scene of a Peaceful Haven. What JG was about to witness as a living nightmare was about to be revealed, and the waters of the lake outstretched before them, was to deliver this dreaded message.

"Gather round, people," instructed Atohi, "we need to seek permission. So ask the lake to unlock the message that she holds for us. Prepare yourself, JG, as this will not be a pleasing sight. Though, it is something that you need to be aware of and is detrimental to saving planet Earth."

On Atohi's command the Good Tribes People started to chant and sway from side to side in time with their hypnotic chanting, the language they used was unrecognisable to JG, but he found it soothing and easy on the ear.

It was, however, the ancient language of the Whispering Planes. The Lake began to react to their soft melody, her waters began to ripple in time and sequence to the soft chanting. A small whirlpool was formed soon and the waters parted softly.

In the distance, a canoe was heading their way, guided by what looked like a large Snowy Owl. He was the Guardian of the Lake, explained Aranck to JG, he had lived her since the beginning of all time. As legend would have it, he was a soft, kindred spirit and lived at the top of the giant Pine at the edge of the Great Lake with mischievous artic squirrels which kept him company.

The Great Snowy Owl pulled up close to the banks and escorted Atohi, Aranck and JG onto the canoe. No words were spoken between them just a mutual understanding could be sensed in the atmosphere as he set off with his passengers and headed towards the middle of the lake where the water had begun to part.

Gradually, they made their way towards the parting. The water now was stronger and her currents ran deep and fast. The canoe began to rock and sway but stood its ground. The Snowy Owl knew exactly what to do, and guided his boat with strength and confidence.

"Look into the Waters, JG, open your eyes and take heed of what they tell you. Use your Puma strength and accurate vision to witness the scene below," said Atohi.

JG at first could not focus well as the canoe continued to sway as great swells of water were lapping over the sides He regained his balance, *having four legs to stabilise you under these conditions was a great advantage*, he thought to himself.

Then he found his focus, and what he was witnessing was a vast underground world in almost complete darkness. It was constructed primarily of concrete and steel, rather like the city of Hanley, but on a much greater scale, and more congested. Everywhere he looked, there were these rat like creatures, seemingly going about their business, carrying objects to and forth. Then, he recognised them as being the mutant creatures that Gabriel had told him about the other day. Taking a closer look at the hellish vision below, Vamcreepers were now appearing on the scene. These great black birds/bats were circling the murky underground world, cawing relentlessly, as they went about their duties. And duties they did have, slaves of Orbotron. These mutant creatures along with the Ratscorps had been assigned to carry out his evil plans of destruction.

Orbotron, this fiendish alien, would not stop until he had relinquished all power and total control. And now his plans had progressed to world domination under earth's crust, right at the centre of her very core.

"Please, please, make it stop. Make is stop," cried out JG, "I have seen enough," he shrieked as he pulled away from the ghoulish scene below.

"JG, pull yourself together, man!!!" said Aranck. "Although, under the circumstances, I don't blame you. You are right to be so shocked. Awful, is it not????? Just like a scene from your worst nightmare."

Chapter 16

"So, my friends, now we are all clear on what we are up against," announced Atohi. "As I said before, it is not a pretty sight, not a pretty sight at all. If I may explain, this is the world that the Evil Orbotron is slowly but surely constructing. You have seen your planets destruction so far, JG? But Orbotron does not want to stop there. As you have just witnessed, he has his mind set on creating a world below earth, a place of even more darkness. A place where he can hide, where the sun never shines and the birds never sing. If he achieves all this, he will surely continue to dominate and mutate. Basically, this crazy alien will stop at nothing until he has his way. So, it is our job to stop him dead in his tracks and we have the power, courage and knowledge to do so. JG, our new friend, you have been chosen by your world and ours to forefront this most important quest."

"Soon, JG, you must leave us and return home. Then shortly, the time will come for everything that you have learnt and experienced during your time spent with myself, the Good Tribes People and the Wise Wild Wolves of the West, in THE LAND THAT ONCE WAS. This will prove to be the most valuable gift bestowed upon you. Keep the amulet close, trust in your Puma form and believe in yourself."

"I know about your Sailing Boat. And how hard you and your dear father have worked on it. I also know that your parents have no idea about your quest, and you worry about this. I can say to you JG. Fear not, they are your parents and they will understand in time. They will be so proud, I promise you this. Can you see that all these things were meant to happen, finding the boat, meeting Gabriel, discovering the manuscript in the library? All these occurrences lead you to us, and now you are ready to journey forthwith."

"Thank you, Atohi. Thank you for your reassuring words. I am really going to miss you guys. You have shown me a world I didn't even know existed. You and the wolves have shown me a way to live that can only be experienced when you can look so deeply inside yourself and believe that anything is possible. You have given me hope and courage and the pure gift of Mother Earth's teachings that remain forever sacred in the Land that Once Was and the Whispering Planes."

"We will be with you in spirit and heart at all times, JG, keep the Amulet close to your chest, remember its powers."

"Oh, not to forget, I have a surprise for you. When you reach the Lost Island of Sacred Souls, Aranck, in his Mountain Lion form will be waiting for you. I have seen how well you work together, and you have definitely bonded. He will prove to be a most valuable guide and companion, alongside Gabriel and your dear animal friends. I am confident that you have a strong team. There is a lot of trust and respect between you all, and this will be a vital mix for victory against the evil Orbotron and his mutant creations."

"I am coooool with that, I could not have asked for more. It is true, Aranck and I have become good friends."

"So, when do I have to leave?" JG said with a heavy heart. How he had revelled within the company of the Wolves and these knowledgeable people, he felt that he had known them all his life. They were like family to him now.

"You have a whole world to save," said Atohi. "Be strong and we can achieve great things. This is not the first and certainly not the last time you will return to our world. Keep The Faith!!!!!"

With that, Atohi gathered his people together, "Friends," he began, "sadly, JG must return home. Gabriel and the Wolves are expecting us at the foot of the Cascades beyond the Banks of our river. It is here where we will find the vortex within its waters which will safely transport JG and Gabriel back to their dimension in time."

Gabriel waited eagerly with his wolf companions by the Waterfall cascades. JG was so pleased to see him and the Wolves, he hugged each and every one of them, and sincerely hoped that he would be returning one day soon to run with the pack and feel once again as free as a bird.

Harmony reassured him that they would all be together again soon.

"Hey JG, don't forget what you have learnt!" Harmony exclaimed.

"And don't forget how to howl," said Tiger. "Remember how you said your friends back home would be soooo impressed."

"They sure will," said JG. "Thank you all so much for everything. For teaching me the Ways of the Wilderness, and to live in peace with Nature. You are so lucky to live like this every day. Oh and another thing, what a great workout you guys have given me, my body feels re-energised, like new, yeh! Thanks for that."

He then turned towards Atohi and the Good Tribes people. Atohi reached out and touched the Precious Amulet close to JG's chest, he then whispered some ancient words whilst looking towards the sky, threw his strong arms around JG hugging him dearly. Remember, I am sending Aranck with my blessing, he will be there to meet you when you arrive on the shores of the Lost Island of Sacred Souls.

"Yeh!!!!! Man." JG turned to Aranck. "I am counting on you."

"Erupting Super volcanoes and hurricanes could not keep me away. I will be there, don't worry. On one condition though. Remember to bring some of that Rock Music with you."

"Would not go anywhere without it, consider it done," said JG.

With that the Wise Wild Wolves of the West and the Good Tribes People disappeared into the wilderness, leaving JG and Gabriel all alone by the Waterfall Cascades.

Chapter 17

"Well, I guess, that's it then," said JG, wiping a tear away from his eyes homeward bound.

"Yes, that's it for now," said Gabriel looking intently at the young man.

"If you could sum up the whole experience in one word. What would you say?" Gabriel asked inquisitively.

"I would say mind blowing."

"Are you sure that is not two words?" joked Gabriel.

"No. Really, it has been some experience. Now, how do we get back to our dimension? Atohi mentioned something about a Vortex within the Cascades or something?"

"Ah, yes. Leave that up to me. Just keep on track and I will lead the way," Gabriel spoke with assurance in his voice.

With a confident, stride Gabriel entered the Cascade, closely followed by JG.

"Wow, wow!!! This is nice. I expected it to feel cold but it's just like taking a power shower. The temperature is just right, and my muscles all over my body are starting to relax. I could get use to this. Another good reason to return to the Land that Once Was, yes, the Land that Once…" he trailed off.

"JG, JG, it's Mum and Dad, how are you feeling, son? Speak to us, please. Please speak to us. We know you can hear us. Come on, son, come back to us. It's Mum and Dad here, we need and miss you and all your friends have not stopped calling. We are all worried about you. Come on, son. Wake up, wake up."

JG was floating through the cascades but in the distance he could here familiar voices, familiar voices of back home, he could here Jericho barking anxiously, and could sense his mum and dad's sadness. He wanted to reach out to them all, but he felt trapped between the two worlds. And the warm trickling waters from the cascades, just kept on flowing. His muscles were easing off. Although, he felt hazy, he could just make out his bedroom window, and the familiar décor of his room, then he saw a smile a big smile on his mum's face. "Tommy, Tommy, quick," JG's mum called out his dad's name, "he has come back to us. JG, JG, we knew you could do it son. It's Mum and Dad, we are here for you, we love you!!!!!"

Jericho started bounding around the bedroom barking excitedly as JG spoke his first words after his long sleep.

"Mum, Dad," he called out in a whisper.

"Take it easy son, don't get up too soon," his mum gently touched JG's arm.

"Have I been asleep for a long time?"

"Well you could say that son, almost two days. We had to call the emergency doctor. You have been in and out of sleep, and had a high temperature. We have not left your side for all that time."

"Throughout your sleep, you were talking and moving rapidly constantly. At one point, we thought you were howling in pain. The Doctor was rather worried, you were under observation and were being monitored at all times."

"Howling, you say," said JG. "You mean howling like a Wolf?" he said this with a twinkle in his eye, as he cast his mind back to his adventures in the Land That Once Was and the Whispering Planes.

"Like a Wolf, now that you mention it," said JG's mum suspiciously. "You did sound rather like a Wolf," this got JG's mum thinking about her son's special personality again. Although she had no idea, no idea at all, about JG's vision and his visit to the Land that Once Was, she was a mother and mothers have a sixth sense about these things.

"Just get some rest, my dear, and I will bring you up a cup of your favourite homemade tomato soup with crusty bread and butter."

"Wow, Mum. That will hit the spot. By the way, what day is it?"

"It is Friday lunchtime, you mean tomorrow is Saturday? Well, JG, it usually does come after Friday."

"So, if it is Saturday tomorrow that only means one thing. dadadaddadaaaaaaaaa the Boat Fest. I must get up out of bed noooooooooooooowwwwww!!!!!" shrieked JG, "I have so much to do, sooooooo many people to contact. I can't waste any time sipping soup in bed."

"Now, hold on, JG," stepped in JG's dad, "Let's just calm down, shall we? You have not been quite yourself and need to chill for a couple of hours or two. Just lay there, and we will sort everything out."

"But, the Boat Fest, Dad. You don't understand. It just has to go ahead. People and friends are counting on us."

"Let's just get you checked by the Doctor once more, and I will give the go ahead for the Boat Fest, deal?"

"OK, Dad. It's a deal."

Content that JG had agreed to a medical check by the Doctor, his dad left the room to call the surgery. As JG sunk back into his pillow, all that was going through his mind were the events that had just occurred on the other side of the Waterfall Cascades. Now he knew the time, for sure, had come to set sail to the Lost Island of Sacred Souls and hopefully Aranck as promised by Atohi, would be there waiting for him.

But before all this could happen, much work was to be done here at home. The Doctor came and went, he had given JG the all clear stating that he was in tip top condition. And as long as he was invited to the Boat Fest tomorrow, he could see no reason why it could not go ahead.

With that taken care of, JG relished and nourished himself on the bowl of delicious homemade soup. Then he took a quick shower, and got himself ready to the rocking sounds of none other than Galaxy's End which reminded him, he must phone his mate Ricky the Red ASAP.

Jericho watched in amazement. Something about his friend had changed, he seemed all grown up but there was something else about him, and yes, Jericho had picked up on the fact that JG had been in the company of a Wolf pack. She wagged her tail approvingly at this notion.

Lizzy the white canary was happy to be back in JG's company too. She had missed him, and could sense that they were to accompany him on his fated journey soon. He seemed different to her too, but like Jericho, was rather impressed by his, shall we say, wilder personality.

Chapter 18

JG finally got hold of his best friend Ricky. The arrangements were that Ricky the Red and the rest of the gang were to meet up at JG's in precisely one hour's time; with a strict dress code being the Cool Rock look and hairstyles with musical instruments it.

And so they arrived. What a Crew! Ricky the Red, as cool as ever, he had even brought along one of his many guitars. "Well," he said, entering the garden, "who could refuse a little music while we work."

"Yehhhh!!! Nice one!!!!!" said Frank the Prank, he was a hilarious character always up for a good joke, "that's your excuse to get out of some real work."

"Behave, Pranker," said Ricky. "You know, you guys can't resist my rocking tunes," with a confident smirk he turned to his friends and they could not but all, agree.

"OK, guys!!!!!" announced Tommy, "JG's dad, let's get into action. The countdown has officially started. It is now 2pm, Friday afternoon, and the Boat Fest is scheduled for 8pm on Saturday. We have roughly around 100 guests attending."

"With maybe, who knows, a few gate crashers!" exclaimed Frank the Prank.

"Possibly, we hope not," said Dad.

"No worries, Mr, check out these muscles," said Frank. "I'm your man, if things get a little difficult."

"Nice one!!!" said Dad. "Have no fear while Frank is here."

Putting all jokes aside for the time being, on a more serious note, a couple of mutants have been lurking in the shadows in the form of a Vamcreeper and a Ratscorp. And yes, young readers, they have been sent by the Evil Orbotron. These mutant spies of the murky skies and the underworld have all the information they need so far, and will now return to their master to report what they have just heard.

Orbotron eagerly awaits the return of his mutant creations. As every day passes, he becomes a little more anxious. And as we already know, he is greedy for total power and hopes to finish his underground world by the end of the year.

His already low patience threshold is wearing thin and his temper is becoming more exaggerated as he becomes more aware of JG's intentions to rescue the planet and turn his plans upside down.

"How could a young boy meddle with my master plan? This has literally been over 300 years in the making. I am a respected leader throughout the galaxy, feared by many, and now, this young human boy comes on the scene and thinks he can take it all away from me. Let him try, just let him try," thunders Orbotron the Silver Oval, shudders with his voice as he impatiently awaits the return of his mutants. He is nervous and angry, he knows that this is a feeling he cannot cope with. He paces the halls of the great Atrium, is he weakening? Has the time come for the Great Orbotron to be over thrown?

Just as he is about to crack with impatience, the Vamcreeper and the Ratscorp return with news, for their master.

"Well! Well! Well! What have you both got to report?" His soulless black eyes narrowed in their large sockets as he prepared to listen to their story.

It is the Vamcreeper who glides forward and is first to tell all. He begins with a nervous squawk, "Master, prepare yourself for what you are about to hear. It appears that the young boy is more gifted than we had ever imagined. Let's just say, he certainly has friends in higher places. Friends that are not of this dimension."

"Explain yourself, crow!!!!!" boomed Orbotron impatiently as his eyes narrow even more intensely. "Are you aware of the boy's connection to the Wolf Dog Gabriel?"

"Yes, you have already informed me of this after your trip to the Library the other day. When you tried but failed to seize the ancient manuscript," Orbotron snapped back viciously. "We are old enemies, and I have been aware of the Wolf Dog's presence for some time."

"Well this, Gabriel Wolf Dog creature, turns out to be the boy's Guardian Angel. He has connections with other world dimensions. Legend has it that this dimensional world is known as the Land that Once Was and is guarded by the Wise Wild Wolves of the West and the Good Tribes People of The Whispering Planes who practice the ancient art of shape shifting and are as one with Nature and Mother Earth."

"The Good Tribes People reside in a sacred place on the banks of a wide life nurturing river, and the Wolves live in the Wild Woods of the West. Both these groups; united together, make up what is known throughout history as the Lords of Nature. The young boy has visited their lands in the form of a vision guided by Gabriel. He has spent time with them and gained their extensive knowledge."

"Therefore, the consequence of JG joining forces with the Lords of Nature has strengthened the bond between the earth of this dimension and spirit Mother Earth who will offer protection, who is, after all, Planet Earth's Guardian."

"So, in other words, you are trying to tell me we are not just dealing with a young boy. We are dealing with powerful spiritual forces from another dimension and time?" exclaimed Orbotron even more deflated and with a hint of defeat in his oppressive tone.

"I am afraid my master that, sadly, it is the case. To you, oh great one, I only speak the truth."

Orbotron was for a short time lost for words, as he quietly went over to his chair in the centre of the Atrium. He seemed to be in some kind of a trance, as he pulled his silver cloak more tightly around his spindly frame. Just for a second, the wicked alien appeared fragile and lost.

Then, without notice, he shot up from his seat. Raising his arms above his head and raising his voice at the same time, "I am the Great Orbotron, no such fools can outwit me, we will soon see who will be the overall Victor. Mark my words!" he protested.

"Going back to your report, any more news on the current situation? For example, what plans have been made recently?" the alien continued to probe.

"There was some mention of a Boat Fest to launch the Sailing Boat, that JG and his father had found washed up on the shores of the city port," answered the Vamcreeper nervously. He was becoming a little wary of the alien, and was expecting an outburst from his master at any point.

"Is this still going ahead, do you know?" the alien continued to probe further.

"Ah, yes. Yes, indeed, Great Orbotron," grunted the Ratscorp as he scurried forward edging closer towards his master.

"I do believe a party is scheduled for tomorrow evening, and yes, I can confirm that it will be a Boat Fest. This is a form of a celebration to launch the shipwrecked, sailing boat. It has been restored to a very high standard, very modern and luxurious, and fitted with the most up to date technology. Even a great technological wizard like yourself, Sir, would be impressed with it," The Ratscorp continued, he was quite proud of himself discussing important news with the great Orbotron, he licked his long whiskers and waited patiently for a response from the alien.

"Um, UMMMMMMM," Orbotron thought on tapping his large head with his spindly fingers.

"So, I presume, this young boy has intentions to use this boat. And I am guessing he will be using it very soon, if I am not mistaken. He has the map of the Lost Island, and the Manual. And as you know, for many centuries, I have been searching for both of these, but sadly, to no avail. If only! If only! I could get my hands on this Manual and the Map, Earth's Last Hope would be crushed forever," his voice reached some great heights again, as the alien boomed out his words. "She would be doomed for all eternity, under my powers, until the end of all time."

This last outburst seemed to have weakened Orbotron a little, as he once again stumbled over to his chair, and sat down gasping for air. Grasping his cloak ever more tightly around his tall, thin frame.

After a short pause the alien had calmed himself down somewhat and was impatient once again to carry on with his demands.

"Vamcreeper," he then spoke with a quieter tone, "I need you to summon the security guards. Nowwww!!!!! Tell them to come and see me. We have a lot of work to do, which will take some planning before tomorrow evening."

Then he looked towards the Ratscorp. Narrowing his eyes, he said, "you stay here with me and let's chat some more about this sailing boat, shall we?"

"Yes, master, anything you want, master," the Ratscorp answered enthusiastically, the strange beast scurried a little closer towards Orbotron.

Chapter 19

Presently, clumsy footsteps could be heard from outside the Atrium as the Security Guards were preparing themselves for the proposed meeting. (As you may know, readers, these poor guards are really the Rock Band Galaxy's End but have been put under a cruel hypnotic spell by the evil Orbotron).

"Ahhhhh!!!!! Men, yes, just the people I have been waiting for," shrieked Orbotron as he raised himself upwards from his chair, this time he seemed to be floating and was elevated a little off the ground as he moved in closer to the expecting Security Guards.

"As I am an impatient soul and greedy for success, I shall begin without further ado. First, let us make ourselves more comfortable," as he beckoned them into a side room which was simply furnished with a large meeting room style table and equipped with steel high backed chairs. The room had a wonderful view of the City of Hanley but outside the skies were grey. A flock of Vamcreepers could be sighted close by circling the Silver Oval on guard as they had been instructed to do so.

Once all were seated, the Great Orbotron spoke; still elevated as he loomed over the guards. His presence grew even more menacing by the day. His evil, pitch black eyes in their large sockets had taken on a reddish hue around the outer rims as they darted like snakes tongues around the room.

"Well, shall I begin? All sitting comfortably?????" he spoke with a sarcastic tone, "Men, I have summoned you all here today to inform you that our mission has officially started as of nowwwwww!!!!!" he boomed again, sending shock waves of sound around the room, the poor security guards did not know what had hit them.

Eddie Eezzie rose to his feet, clutching his head in his hands. He had a quick temper and good easily jump to the defence of his fellow band members.

"Be cool man!!!!! We are not a million miles away, we are here in this room. You almost blew all our heads off with your booming voice."

"Be quite and sit down," shouted back Orbotron, as he could not stand to be challenged especially by a mere human. "I have not given you the word to speak. Just listen to my instructions. A plan must immediately be put into action, and you men are going to help me with it," *little do they know that they are under my hypnotic spell, and will do whatever I say*, he chuckled to himself, rubbing his spindly hands together, *What fools!!!!!*

"I will go on. Tomorrow evening at 8 pm, this boy, JG's parents and friends are holding a Boat Fest party. And you men in your rock status form will be performing at this said party and will once again become the famous Rock Group Galaxy's End. All the while you will still be under my spell and I will have full control of your brain activities, thanks to my super intelligence and my MMM Computer system, which, if you care to know, stands for Max Minding Mentoring Computer System."

"So, while you are performing, singing and playing your little hearts out to masses of adoring fans, you will be sooooo unaware of your hypnotic state. Through your eyes, I will be able to capture the whole scene to ascertain and obtain JG's plans. Practically, you will become more secret spies. I, as always, will be under total control," he laughed an evil laugh and his whole body took on an even more sinister stance.

"I, the Great Orbotron, will be adding the finishing touches to my master plan. And you, my men, are the cherry on the cake, the snowcap on the mountain top. You Galaxy's End, are my tools to success. Most unfortunately, for you guys, you will be none the wiser to what I have just said. At this very moment, I am programming you to follow all my instructions. Therefore, in 10 seconds, this meeting will terminate and well, let's just say, it has never even taken place in your minds."

"Ten, nine, eight, seven, six, five, four, three, two2, one. Open your eyes!!!!!"

The bewildered security guards, a little shaken and with pounding heads, looked at one another totally unaware of what had happened. Just has he had predicted, Orbotron looked on (*like putty in my hands (as you humans say*), his evil eyes narrowing with triumphant greed, ohhhhh!!! How he revelled about being in control! It was, of course, what he was born to do.

But no!!! Eddie Eezzie was not going down that easily. For some time now he had just been playing along with Orbotron's sick game. And by some miracle, he had become immune to the alien's evil doings, quick-witted and as sharp as a knife. When duty calls and the time is right, he will know when to fight back. You don't call this chap a True Rocker for nothing, you know!!!

Eddie Eezzie had to be careful not to show too much attitude or he may blow his cover. He was an intelligent chap and quickly understood what he was dealing with. A Megalomaniac Alien with a massive ego!!!!! Even bigger than his own, and now that was saying something!!!!! I think that sums up Orbotron pretty well. Don't you, readers?

Chapter 20

So now Eddie knew the alien's next steps. With this knowledge, Eddie was fast becoming quite an important character in the story. He had been thrown into the mix. In fact, his knowledge would prove to be vital over the coming hours. He must get an urgent message through to JG and alert him of Orbotron's intentions.

Thinking aloud, Eddie said, "Wait. So if today is Friday, what time would it be?????" turning to Lex the Lizard, his electric guitarist in the band.

He answered, "It's getting on for 5.00 pm man, and I will be clocking off my shift in just under half an hour."

"Great, nice one," said Eddie. "OK. So, 5.00 pm," Eddie repeated back the time to himself, "and I don't clock off for another five hours, I am stuck here until 10.00pm. Quick, think Eddie. Think (he said speaking to himself) you need to alert JG, from this point onwards. Time is precious."

"If only I could just get to my mobile phone. But, no. Then I would have to come up with some excuse to come off duty and go down to the personnel locker rooms. And considering how paranoid Orbotron is, he has eyes and mutant creatures everywhere, it would certainly raise some uninvited superstition. No, there has to be another way around this."

"Now, think. Eddie, think," speaking to himself again. "If you can compose number one Rock hits, you can surely come up with a prior warning to alert a friend."

"Ah, yes. Got it, got it. Lexxxxx, Lex, the Lizard. That's it! He must go and forewarn them." He had to be quick though. Lex the Lizard was not called the Lizard for nothing. He was as quick as a whippet and would be leaving the building with much haste. This man did not know what going slow meant. After some thought, the best way to get Lex's attention would be to use the walkie-talkie system.

Thankfully, the walkie-talkie idea worked. In a matter of seconds, Lex was by his side. Now, although, Lex was still under Orbotron's spell, he still had some capacity to be able to carry out favours and instructions from other people. He may get a little confused along the way but he was the only choice in this situation to relay the message to JG.

Eddie, so as not to confuse Lex, realised he must keep the message simple and to the point. "OK, Lex, this is what I want you to do. You need not question this, just merely as my longtime friend carry out this huge favour for me, OK! With me still?????"

"Yes, I am with you, man!!!!! Tell me what I have to do, dude?"

"OK, you must go to JG's house, and tell him that tomorrow evening during the Festival he must keep his eyes peeled for some unexpected and uninvited guests. Tell him that these uninvited guests are enemies that he is, I presume, already well aware of. He should be able to read between the lines of what this message involves, I can only, but have faith in this, hope that Lex my mate can deliver the message safely to JG." (Thus being the thoughts of Eddie.)

"Right, Man. I will do it. No questions asked, Man, I will just go and simply tell him what you have just told me."

"That's right Lex, nice one, I knew I could rely on you."

"Just one thing that I would like to add Lex, this will all seem a lot clearer in time. And all will be explained to you and the rest of the band, OK?" Eddie could not help but feel compassion for his friend's present state of mind.

With that, Lex was off. And like I said before, he was as quick as a Whippet.

Meanwhile back at JG's place, things were coming together and going according to plan for the Boat Fest.

What a great team they all made. The stage was up where Galaxy's End were to perform, they had even laid down a temporary dance floor; complete with party banners, balloons, streamers and lightsabers. It was going to go rockingly well.

As they went about their chores, the atmosphere was cool, tinged with big bursts of excitement in anticipation for the big event. Everyone chatted while they worked, JG could not help but feel so proud at what wonderful friends and parents he had. His thoughts, though, were marked by sadness as he knew tomorrow was the fateful day: SUNDAY 1st JULY 2050. The day he would have to leave his mum and dad. These feelings could only provoke dread and sorrow inside, as the hours ticked by under a whirlwind of preparations and high expectations.

Far in the distant corner, secluded under a bush at the end of the garden, the Wolf Dog Gabriel waited always on alert and ready for action. He had truly found his purpose in life, and had come a long way from an abandoned street dog to this. He felt so blessed to be appointed as JG's guardian, it was such a great honour for him to be living this moment. He fully understood his responsibilities to the young boy.

Gabriel's keen intuition and wolf like nature could sense JG's sadness, but he knew deep down, he would pull through and truly believed that soon they would all be celebrating in the success of their forthcoming journey and the liberation of planet earth. After all, JG had learnt from the best, their friends from the other dimension, who are closer than what we had first thought.

Meanwhile, Lex the Lizard was right on schedule and soon to arrive at JG's. He had made the journey across town in record time. All he had in his head, at this point, was to deliver the message safely to JG, "Ask no questions and query, nothing," he kept repeating to himself, as he entered the garden gate arriving at his destination.

Lex mildly recognised where he was as he had been to JG's before, with Eddie's cousin Ricky, who had spotted Lex straight away and was now approaching him.

"Hey, Lexxy Lizard, my man!" called out Ricky the Red "You are a day early for the Fest. Great to see you though. All set for tomorrow, then??? How is Eddie and the rest of the band? We are so looking forward to hearing you perform."

"Yes, us and about another hundred plus people," called out Frank the Prank.

Lex, under his present state of mind, was totally confused by these questions. But as promised to Eddie, he just kept thinking to ask no questions and query nothing so he nodded accordingly.

"I have a message from Eddie actually for JG, is he around by any chance????? Yes, man. He is just over there," Ricky said. "What's up, man? You just don't seem yourself, are you ok?"

"Yes, no worries, mate. I am fine, just need to pass this message on to JG and then I must leave."

"Right, cool, will just go and get him for you." Ricky the Red at this point was becoming quite suspicious. He had known Lex for some time and he was definitely showing signs of some acute weirdness, he thought to himself. *Well, I hope he is OK. Poor guy, he is such a talented guitarist.*

JG made is way over to the awaiting Lex, "Hi Lex, I believe you have a message for me from Eddie?"

"Yep, sure do!!!!! And here goes, keep your eyes peeled tomorrow night for some unexpected and uninvited guests. These are enemies that you are very well aware of," Lex repeated the words parrot fashion as instructed by Eddie.

"OK, got that?" asked Lex.

"Got it and before you ask; yes, it does make sense, so thanks. Tell Eddie that I have got it covered. Thanks man!"

"Sure you don't want to stick around for a while Lex? Get yourself a drink or something?????"

"Thanks, but no thanks, I must be getting off now!!!!!"

"OK, see you tomorrow," said JG. "For the BIG BLAST!"

"Um, see you tomorrow then," answered Lex, still confused as to what possibly could be going on. He left the group of guys busy at their work.

Great!!!!! Problems before I even set sail tomorrow, thought JG as he mulled over the words and message that had just been delivered by Lex. "Funny though!!!!! How could Eddie know what I was involved in," it puzzled him greatly as he could just not see the connection.

He knew he could trust Eddie, he had known him from a small child. After all he was Ricky's older cousin, and they had always been friends. But he could not understand where Eddie had come by this information, and could he possibly know about what JG was about to embark on, and the past events that he had been involved in.

"Um… the plot certainly does thicken," JG thought and spoke it out loud to himself.

"What did you just say, mate?????" quizzed Ricky.

“Oh, sorry!!! I was just thinking out aloud.”

“Nooo, not you as well, JG, not another guy acting strange, and going all vague on me. Just what we need before the Boat Fest!!!”

Ricky could not conceal his concern any longer, and had to ask what the message was that Lex had just delivered.

“No worries, Ricky. I have got it covered. It was just a message from Eddie to say… well, it is a secret really. You will find out tomorrow night.”

“But none of this is making any sense, why did Eddie or Lex just not simply call us????? Why send Lex in person to tell you something????? Come on, after all we are living in the year 2050, has no one around here heard of AAMS. Advanced Accurate Mobile Systems????? The science is in the name,” Ricky was becoming more concerned by the hour.

“It’s just getting a little strange around here,” Ricky the Red could sense a mystery unfolding, something was about to materialise, involving his best mate JG, and perhaps even his cousin Eddie, and once he got on those tracks and that train of thought, he could not let go. Our Ricky was a persistent fellow.

JG could see his friend deeply in thought and his mind was all over the place, he was literally like the old saying a terrier with a bone.

He wanted so much to confide in his friend but how could he. If he did, then tomorrow would surely never happen. He would not be able to set sail. His mum and dad would find out and all hope would be lost in time. Orbotron would win the day and his evil curse would continue without end. No! He must keep quiet and just focus on tomorrow.

To take his mind off the strange happenings of the day, Ricky decided that they were all in need of some Musical Therapy, so as the evening wore on and they had nearly accomplished everything that was needed for the Fest. Ricky the Red announced that he was going to provide them with a musical treat. Considering they had all worked their little socks off, they were entitled to a ‘Session of Sound’ as he put it. “Gather round guys and let me entertain you!!!!!”

Placing himself on the stage, he rip roared into musical action with his electronic guitar. How he could rock those tunes, his voice was not too bad either. Everyone lost themselves in the music including JG's mum and dad. They all got up on the stage and joined in with a few rock classics.

Then Dad called an end to the jamming session, "Come on, guys, now let's quit while we are ahead. After all, we need to save our energies for the Biggie tomorrow night." The happy crowd decided to call it a night and retired to bed peacefully.

Gabriel, that night, had the company of Jericho. The Husky dog had sniffed out Gabriel's hiding place and decided to go and bed down next to him. *It would be cool to sleep under the stars, with practically a real-life wolf*, she had thought. Gabriel was glad of Jericho's presence; he had secretly grown quite fond of this dashing lady. He proceeded to tell her his life story from the beginning, when he was just a pup and had been granted a home with a human companion. Jericho listened with interest as the story unfolded into the night.

Chapter 21

No sooner had JG hit the pillow, it was Saturday morning 30th June 2050, the day of the Boat Fest had finally arrived. And what a beautiful summer day it was. There was not a cloud in the sky. For some reason, the murkiness that was usually present had seemingly been replaced by sun and blue sky. *This is a good omen sent from The Land That Once Was and the Whispering Planes*, thought JG, *Spirit Mother Earth is sending us a message disguised in the weather that all will be fine.*

Enthusiastically, he jumped out of bed ready to take on the day and what a day it will be. Young Readers are you ready to be dazzled????? I think we have a party to attend!!!!! Shall we???

There was definitely excitement and thrill in the neighbourhood and surrounding areas that day. It was, if a universal spell had been cast and twinning with the good weather, the warm sunshine and the bluest of blue sky, all was at peace with the world, as if anything could be possible, and that feeling carried on into the evening. 8 pm quickly came around and the whole garden was illuminated, it was still warm and the universal buzz could clearly be felt in the fully charged atmosphere. A little after eight the guests steadily started to arrive.

Ricky and the crew had got there early at 5 pm, they had helped JG set up the stage and the acoustics in good time for the arrival of the star guests; Galaxy's End.

The party mood was in full swing, music was rocking out of every sound system rigged up in the garden, delicious food and drinks were already on offer, people started to mingle in an upbeat mood to ravenous young crowd, there was even a few brave ones who had already made it onto the dance floor.

Frank the Prank, as you know, always up for a laugh, had got a group of young girls together to show off their dance skills; dressed for the part and in full dance regalia, these young girls were good friends of the boy's crew and hung out regularly together when the boys had a jamming session. The girls danced while the boys jammed. These young ladies attended the Dance Academy, Shoot for the Stars in the centre of Hanley and had won many a competition covering all aspects of dance, ranging from ballet / hip hop and street dance to contemporary and circus style acrobatics.

Tonight though, seeing as though it was a Rock Party, they had decided to treat their fellow party revellers to a Contemporary Dance piece with the addition of some rather cool circus style acrobatics; they had even brought along their own trapeze, a circus wire, and a small trampoline. "Wow!!!!! We are sure in for a treat," exclaimed JG's mum, who along with Dad was really getting into the swing of things. A few courageous adults namely, some good friends of JG's Parents, the doctor and his girlfriend, were in full party mood too.

The Dance Troup was breath taking, they literally held everyone's attention as they danced and grooved in time with a great rocking piece. Ricky the Red could not contain himself any longer, man. He had to get himself some of the action as he reached for his Electric Guitar, and belted out some crazy rock vibes in time to the dancing girls. They made full use of the circus apparatus and with great flexibility, they articulated their muscular bodies with both skill and accuracy whilst maintaining their elegant postures which had to be put down to years of Classical Ballet training.

"OK now!!!!!" announced Suzie Smooth, the head of the Dance Troup. "We need some volunteers from the crowd and, I think, a gift is in the offering, if you can help us with our next piece. We need a lady actually, so no hard feelings guys, I don't think it would go down very well if you had to put on one of our dance uniforms, now, would it?" as Suzie produced a tight fitting electric blue leotard and silver ballet shoes.

"Hey. Hey, you never know!!!" shouted out none other than Frank the Prank, "I reckon one of those outfits would do my figure some justice, what do you think crowd?????"

At this point the crowd were ecstatic with what Frank had just suggested, and were crying out for him to try it on. "Try it on!!! Try it on!!!" they all screamed and chanted.

"Go on, Son!!!!!" shouted out one of the adults. "Give us a whirl." Without any more encouragement, Frank jumped on stage, swiped the leotard and ballet shoes out of Suzie's hands before she could say the words Dance Mania.

Back flipping off the stage whilst grasping the outfit, our Frank was ready to pull the party beat up a notch or two, and all at his own expense; how he loved to make people laugh and have a great time.

Dressed and ready to go in the dance costume, Frank made his entrance. Forward flipping and pirouetting onto the dance floor, the crowd were silent in anticipation, awaiting his next move.

Frank at se15 years of age was quite a muscular guy. He had a slim build but how he fitted into a size eight's figure hugging leotard was anybody's guess? Whatever he was doing, it was working and he certainly got the party revellers crying out for more as he pulled a young, awaiting girl out of the crowd and proceeded to dance with her.

"Hit it with the music DJ," he announced. The young girl could not help but get swept away by the moment. The crowd was loving it, he picked her up and spun her round as she followed his lead.

What fun!!! They were having.

By this time, the dance floor was quickly filling up as the dance group of girls had encouraged people to join in and get on with the groove. After all, what are Festivals for?

Shortly after nine, JG and Ricky tried to silence the crowd as they were ready to announce the arrival of, wait for it, da-da-da… Yes, you have guessed it, Galaxy's End.

"OK, guys. May I have your attention?" JG spoke into the microphone. "As you know," he proceeded. "Tonight we have some very special guests who will soon be performing for you," (while on stage, he took the opportunity to scan the crowds, as directed in the message from Eddie to see if he could detect any suspicious beings.) *All clear for now*, he thought, phew and double phew!!! As he maintained his cool stance in front of the crowd.

“So, without further ado. It is a great honour in the name of Rock Music to announce the band, Galaxy’s End. Let’s GIVE IT UP FOR GALAXY’S END,” the crowd went wild as the Rock Group led by Eddie took their places on stage.

Rip roaring into action, Eddie with his trademark double forward flip before any performance, thrashed out their number one hit: Sky Surfers.

“Wow!!! He is vocalising well,” exclaimed Ricky the Red as he proudly looked on at his older cousin, one day he dreamed of playing in Eddie’s band.

Lex the Lizard went into full blown Rockers Guitar Mode, Ben Beyond on the Drums was as amazing as ever, he really pelted out the beat with such energy and rhythm and on Keyboards was Sean Shore Sharky, commonly known as the dude with the cutest smile in the band, this being the general opinion of his girlie admirers.

Let’s face it now the four of them together were just mind blowing!!! Amazing!!! They were Galaxy’s End.

Chapter 22

But midst all these celebrations, just to darken the mood, da, da, da yes, yes, you have guessed it; Orbotron and his mutants were not so far away. In fact, unbeknown to the revelling crowds, Vamcreepers were fast JG's house destination, the tower block of flats flat that towered over his garden and to complete the mutant team Ratscorps were also on the war path, as they gathered themselves together in a secret hiding place which was in close vicinity to the Festival.

The two groups of mutants were Orbotron's eyes and ears; he had designed them that way. They could carry out every element when it came to his complex demands.

The life-sucking alien had positioned himself in a vacant flat inside the tower block as it had an excellent view of the garden. He couldn't have found a better hiding place if he had fallen over it. "How clever am I!" he shrieked, "things just seem to fall into place for me," he crooned to himself with delight.

That crazy alien was so disillusioned, only his inflated ego kept him one step ahead, for now. Time would only be the judge of that.

With menace and as always evil intent at his core, he instructed his chief Vamcreeper Black Sun to be at the forefront of the mission. He would act as prime witness to all that was happening down below in the festival garden and relay the finest of details straight back to the eagerly awaiting Orbotron.

"As far as I can make out, Master," the Vamcreeper cawed back in response, "your security guards, aka Galaxy's End have just arrived on stage and are ready to perform."

"Oh, really now! Ummmmmm… those fools, they think they are successful Rock stars, do they? They are still, and for as long as I require their services, those men will remain under my MMM (Maximum Mind Mentoring) hypnotic spell. Ah, ah, ah!!!!!" he exclaimed with a demonic tone and look to match as he rubbed his pointy chin with his long spindly fingers.

Orbotron continued to relay his instructions to Black Sun, "so, therefore, once they start to play and the crowds are all eyes and ears on the band, we must take our chance and send in the Ratscorps, you must instruct the Vamcreeper Black Knight to lead the Ratscorps into action, their job being to distract the party revellers in whatever way they can, and then Black Knight's job is to track down the sailing boat. Once he has discovered where it is, Black Knight will be instructed by me to install my TTT Device, in other words, my Telepathic Technological state-of-the-art Tracking device. This piece has been over five years in the making, it is so powerful and could detect any object quite easily in outer space, obviously designed by me. I have through scientific procedures installed into its system my very own brain cells, which have connected and moulded together with an advanced wiring system that can only be found on the Mother Planet of Mutraculon."

"As this clever device contains my silver matter, (i.e. Orbotron's brain cells in other words). I can quite literally control it from the comfort of my laboratory, visualising the boat's journey as if I was there myself, you could call it rather like a virtual reality experience. JG and his crew have no chance of victory while the Great Orbotron is at large!!!!!" Mega-inflated ego at large too!!!!! Check this out, young readers.

"So, Black Sun, do I make myself clear, are you and your flock capable of accomplishing this task?????"

"Yes master, of course. Great master, have we ever let you down?"

"Don't push me to gratify you Black Sun, much work is to be done before any gratifications are due, now enough of this. Be gone. Here, take the TTT device, keep this masterpiece safe and under your wing. Make sure you brief Black Knight with my installation instructions, and keep those Ratscorps focused and under control. Got it!!!!!"

"Got it master."

With that Black Sun swooped up the device carefully storing it under his extensive wingspan and took to the sky. What a backdrop! The moon and stars illuminating the night as the eerie figure of the bird creature made its descent in the direction of JG's garden.

Before he could say TTT, Black Knight was immediately at his side and as instructed Black Sun briefed his fellow Vamp and precariously handed over the tracking device, "guard this with your life Black Knight. Without this, the likes of us and our Great Master's Empire are truly doomed," carefully taking it from his mentor Black Knight proudly puffed out his chest. He so wanted to prove to the flock that he was worthy of this special task, and perhaps cunningly take the limelight away from Black Sun.

The Ratscorps were quickly pulled into rank, "enough of your chattering," bellowed Black Sun, "listen carefully and listen well. If you value your future on this planet," his beady eyes scanning each and every one of the Ratscorps, until they were silenced into submission.

By this time Galaxy's End were in full concert mode, so Black Sun seized his chance to commence.

"Troops at the ready, please. Ratscorps, at all times, you must keep your eyes on Black Knight and follow his instructions, keep together. You know your job is to distract the party revellers while Black Knight tracks down the sailing boat. Once he is inside the boat, A rank must keep guard and alert him of any danger if needs be, and B rank must continue to distract the revellers. Pull out all the stops to confuse and frighten them, so that means lots of teeth, claws and scorpion tail action. OK, with that said, we will commence the mission."

Black Knight pulled in the ranks and took the lead flying low to the ground whilst heading in the direction of the house.

Chapter 23

Music booming, young people dancing, the party surely was in full swing. Everyone was having a real rocking time, Galaxy's End were not letting anybody down. Their performance was rip roaring electrifying, they played with such enthusiasm that you would never have guessed they were under some hypnotic trance. Eddie Eezzie felt so proud of them and was desperate to help his friends overcome this mind-altering spell. But first, they must overthrow Orbotron and he knew that JG was the guy to do just that.

For now, though all he could do was to follow Orbotrons orders. He obviously had to bide his time, and get some communication over to JG as soon as the time was right. This wasn't going to be easy as we all know Orbotron had eyes and ears all over the place in the form of his mutant spies.

Then all of a sudden talking about mutant creatures, Eddie Eezzie amidst all the fun, loud music and partying noticed something very suspicious from the corner of his eye, a troop of rat creatures scurrying along in unison heading in the direction of the Boat Shed. *That's strange,* he thought to himself. He had seen one or two of these mysterious creatures about the city by now, and he had also heard about all the reports that were coming in about the strange sightings. He had even seen a couple of them hanging around the Silver Oval, could they be something to do with Orbotron's sick plan?

He quizzed himself (all these thoughts were going through his head as he remained singing his heart out and entertaining the crowd). It was enough Hanley had to put up with the Vamcreepers, he thought on, but now these. There were literally 100s of them, they were bound to be more????? They must have something to do with Orbotron for sure, I can sense him nearby.

With not a moment to lose, he immediately halted the band to stop playing he ceased singing and cried out to the crowd, "RATSCORPBREAKOUT! RATSCORP BREAKOUT! DER, DER, DER, DER, THERE'S A RATSCORP BREAKOUT!!!!!"

Was it part of the act or was there really a Ratscorp breakout? The confusion on the faces of the crowd was apparent as Eddie continued to shout out Ratscorp Breakout, with rhythm still in his voice, as if he was singing it. Quickly, the crowd caught on that it was indeed a real warning, as a number of guests had caught sight of the strange creatures too!!!

All of sudden a sea of panic took hold of the party atmosphere. Some of the young girls were horrified by the scene and had started to scream out loud, "Rats, rats, yuk, rats all over the place," this loud screeching noise caused the mutant rat creatures to panic as they broke ranks and started to mingle and scurry into the already frenzied crowd. Black Knight had caught wind of this but he could not stop. He had arrived at the boat shed, he had to implant the TTT device or his life would not be worth living, and the humiliation of not being able to carry out the procedure would be too much to bear. He simply must get the device implanted. To hell with those useless Ratscorps he would see the job through to the bitter end.

Once inside the Boat Shed, he scanned the area to make sure he was alone. Once he was quite satisfied, he swooped over to the boat. There she was in all her splendour. A moonbeam had squeezed itself through a crack in the roof and had illuminated her decks and magnificent masts. She sure was a beautiful piece of maritime craftsmanship.

It did not take the cunning Vamcreeper long to find the control room where he had been instructed to plant the device. At this crucial point, as if by magic, Orbotron through telepathic means took over with the installation procedure directing the Vamcreeper. As for the device, through some strange science, had somehow connected to its master. Orbotrons destructive mind was therefore at work, making sure that his creation was well and truly up and running and ready for action. The timer was set to go into drive/track mode as soon as the boat hit the seas tomorrow morning.

All secure and in place, Black Knight was overcome by relief. *Don't fail now,* he thought to himself, *job's not over yet.*

He knew that somewhere in close vicinity Black Sun would be waiting for news amongst the shadows.

As for Orbotron, still tucked away in the apartment block, he knew his device was in place as he cunningly snickered to himself with pride and self-admiration. "No wonder this fragile planet has succumbed to my great being. I am just too professional, a true scientist at work," he bellowed.

Outside there was real pandemonium, the Ratscorps had swamped the garden. A frenzy of greed had taken over them, they had quite literally eaten half the buffet, as the frightened guests looked in disbelief.

If they were approached, they would bar their horrific teeth in waning not to come too close. They were much larger than your average rat and with their scorpion-like addition, they certainly raising some hysteria. Jericho could not sit back any longer, she must try and ward off these horrific creatures, but who they really needed, thought Jericho, was Gabriel. He would certainly put a stop to this, and then as if her mind had been read out, he leapt onto the scene. His very size and wolf like presence created a stir straight away with the already half hysterical crowd.

Eddie Eezzie along with JG and Ricky called out for some order, "Friends, friends, our friends. Now, let's just all calm down. We will get this sorted out calmly. The more you panic, the worse it will be," JG looked at Eddie as if to say 'so this is what I had to keep my eyes open for: a Ratscorp invasion which obviously has something to do with Orbotron', yes, he knew it. *They had probably been sent as spies or something*, JG thought to himself.

"Gabriel, Gabriel." JG looked around for the Wolf Dog, who was by his side in a second. "What do you think? These mutants have surely been sent by Orbotron to spy on us?"

"Most definitely JG, without a doubt, I can also sense a flock of Vamcreepers in close vicinity. If they attack, and considering how many they are, we are going to need reinforcements."

Above all the chaos, Eddie found five minutes to confide in JG about Orbotron and how he was and how his band is still under some strange hypnotic mind, controlling spell, conflicted on them by Orbotron. JG could quite not believe what he was hearing, but knew that Eddie would not be fooling around with him, especially over something as important as this.

"JG, I must talk to you later. It is a Matter of Urgency. When we have sent these mutants on their way and the party is over, there is something else I need to tell you. Please, you must listen to me and I will explain."

"Of course, Eddie, you and Ricky are true friends. Friends forever, we will talk soon. First, let's round up these pesky rats and send them packing back to the sewers."

Gabriel and Jericho took the lead in rounding up the mutants. Although it came at a price, these things were vicious. And certainly put up a good fight; teeth snarling, claws outstretched and ready to do battle, they were quick too. They jumped and scurried around the stage and dance floor, still hungrily grabbing food, if they got a chance. Scaring most of the girls boys out of their wits, although, these cool party guys would not care to admit their fear they started to help in fighting back. The rats, grabbing hold of anything they could find, chairs, tables, a couple of garden brooms. What a frenzied sight!!!!!

Ricky then came up with a brilliant plan, "let's hose them down, shall we? Quick. Grab that hose over there and flood them out. The strength of the water should be enough to send them packing, plus, it will cool us down too!" As the evening had worn on, it seemed to have gotten hotter and with all the dancing and craziness, the atmosphere was practically at boiling point, a hot balmy summer night, the last night In June 2050. It was surely going out with a bang, and some unexpected party guests had given it a crazy final ending.

Gabriel and Jericho had done a great job in rounding up these gate crashing rats. They had them cornered and Ricky was ready with the giant garden hose. "Now," shouted out Ricky, giant hose in hand, "prepare to be blasted into outer space, you dingy party poopers!!!!!"

The strong jet of water seemed to be doing the trick as it took the uninvited guests by surprise, JG's dad came to the rescue with another hose which was a lot bigger and more powerful. At this point, the rats did not stand a chance. They were being water blasted from every angle, they had no alternative but to scarper and scarper they did. As quick as they had arrived, the troops of mutant rats left the party scene soaked right through to their scrawny bodies. Off they scampered defeated and deflated back in the direction of the Silver Oval and to suffer, no doubt, Orbotron's Wrath.

"Well, we did it," said Tommy, JG's dad. "That was some unsuspecting ending if ever there was one," he commented.

"Yep, success! That saw those little devils off exclaimed Eddie and I think, just to round off the evening on a more successful note, we have just about enough time for another track before the end of the Fest as it was fast approaching midnight. "

Chapter 24

Eddie somersaulted onto the stage. *Where that guy gets his energy from was anybody's guess, but he sure was fun, a true performer*, thought JG.

"OK, party goers, I think after all that upheaval and rat business, just to seal the night on a Rocking note, we, Galaxy's End are going to play you out with an old favourite of ours and I think you will agree too. We are going to perform for you our hit 'WORLD CLASS HERO'."

The crowd was ecstatic once again as they switched from all partied out mode to all party in mode in a matter of seconds. What a song to end off the night in style!

Lex the Lizard on the guitar, Ben Beyond on the Drums and Shaun Shore Sharky on the Keyboards came together along with Eddie to prove that they were a Musical Legend.

So it was official, The Boat Fest was a big, big, bumper success.

A pang of sadness now crept over JG as he said goodbye to all his guests. Little did they know that they would not be seeing him again for some time, and worst of all, the idea of leaving his parents came to mind like a bolt of lightning striking a tower block. With adrenalin pumping through his veins, he went to find his mates to say goodbye. And then he must meet up with Eddie as he sensed his information would prove to be crucial for the journey ahead.

"Guys, well what do you think? Did we give them a good time?"

"Yes, we did," they all shouted in unison.

"JG, the Fest will be talked about for months, it was awesome," said Ricky

"I could not have done it without you lot. Come on, group hi-five." They really were a close group of friends, he was going to miss these guys. These were his best mates, and they had no idea of JG's departure. "Catch you all tomorrow then, guys!" exclaimed Ricky, "How about a jamming session round at my place?"

"Yes, sounds cool!" they all agreed. Just then Ricky's dad pulled up in his Jeep to take them all home.

JG sat down exhausted. All that kept him focused now was to succeed, he had no time for sentiment, he had to fight for what is right. He cast his mind back to the Land That Once Was, the Good Tribes People and the Wise Wild Wolves of the West. They were with him all the way, he could feel it deep down in his soul. He knew would never face this battle alone.

He stared out into the night and caught sight of a group of fireflies making the most of the warm weather, he watched them for a while dancing and weaving in and out of his mum's Prize Olive Tree, and then he heard them; familiar voices, voices from the Whispering Planes and the Wild Woods, calling his name urging him to be strong and to keep the faith. "The Amulet, the Amulet, it was Atohi's voice that whispered through the olive leaves, JG, keep it close to your chest as I instructed, close to your heart at all times and you will not fail, I promise you this, my Friend!!!"

What comforting words he spoke, Gabriel had picked up on this and settled down next to JG, resting his head on his knees. "Come on, JG, you need your rest. We have a big day tomorrow."

"I need to catch Eddie a moment, he has something important he needs to tell me," the band was nearly all packed up as JG approached Eddie, intriguingly.

"JG, what I am about to tell you may be a little shocking so prepare yourself for what you are about to hear. All I can tell you and you have to believe me is that I am on your side with all my heart."

"I will begin tomorrow, I know you are to set sail destination to some Long Lost Island in the wide open seas. I know this because for the last year or so, I and Galaxy's End have been trapped under Orbotron's hypnotic mind spell. He has had us all working for him as security guards over at the Silver Oval, one by one through some telepathic trick, he has managed to gain partial access to our brains and can control our very thoughts and actions."

"Unbeknown to him and miraculously, I am no longer under his telepathic control. I have managed to break free from this cursed spell. And I am once again my own person. I wish I could say so for the rest of the band, it aches my heart to see them like this."

JG was shocked and it took some time to mull this over, then he spoke, "Wow, man!!!!! That's pretty shocking to hear, obviously, our evil alien friend has no idea that you are free from his spell?"

"Naaaa, no idea at all!!! I keep that cleverly disguised and just go along with his wishes until the time is right to fight back."

"Now you have the history. Here comes the important part; Orbotron has placed a tracking device somewhere in the control room on your boat. When you leave for the seas tomorrow, we are to follow you, along with a flock of Vamcreepers and a pack of Ratscorps We will be under constant surveillance by Orbotron as he controls us from his underground laboratory within the Silver Oval."

"You see, his overall plan is to stop you discovering the secrets that the Lost Island holds. If you do discover them, however, as I am probably sure you may know, you can overthrow him and Planet Earth can breathe once again. Her natural beauty will be restored and harmony will be bequeathed upon our World."

"That, Eddie, is what I, and some special friends intend to do," as he spoke these words of truth he touched the Amulet and the Faith was all there.

"Good Luck, JG, and don't forget I am on your side until we meet again," and with that Eddie rounded up his band and their instruments and like his friends. They disappeared into the night. What a night it was! 12.30pm and still warm, there was not a single cloud to be seen, only a blanket of stars and the moon, of course.

"The boat!!!" JG jumped up and exclaimed, "We have forgotten one vital thing, THE BOAT!!!!! How on earth are we going to get the boat down to the port!!!!!"

Gabriel could hear panic in his voice. "JG relax, chill. Let us just say that good forces from another dimension are going to take care of that for us. All you need to do now is concentrate on getting in some hours of shut eye. Myself and Jericho will remain here with the boat until the early hours."

"Just rest, my friend. Just rest, and close your eyes."

That night, sleep came easily to JG and the last words he heard were the soothing sounds of Gabriel. He closed his eyes and slept.

Part 2

Chapter 25

1st July 2050 – 9.00 am – the high seas somewhere in the middle of the ocean.

Destination – The Long Lost Island of Sacred Souls.

JG woke up to the aroma of salty air, on an undulating bed; a comfy bed, none the less. Familiar, yet unfamiliar, Wait! This was not his bed, this was not even his bedroom. *Where on earth, am I?* he thought.

He then had a notion, "Could it be, no! Am I on my boat?????" he spoke out loud to himself.

"You are indeed," whispered Lizzie in his ear.

"Lizzie, you're here!!! Am I dreaming, Lizzie???"

"No, JG, this is real. The room is real. The boat is real, and we are in the middle of the Ocean on your boat."

"But, how!!! I have no recollection of any of this, where is Jericho and Gabriel??? They must be here too."

"Of course they are out on deck, I have been keeping you company while you were sleeping." Then with a bolt of shock out of the blue, JG suddenly remembered his mum and dad.

"Oh no!!!!! Mum and Dad, they will be looking for me by now. They will be out of their minds with worry."

"JG, they are sleeping."

"What do you mean by sleeping? Mum and Dad never lie in and how do you know this when you are hear with me Lizzie?"

"JG, they are safe from worry and stress, they don't even know you have gone. Gabriel will explain properly in a moment, calm yourself down, and come and have a look at the view, through your porthole window." JG edged himself a little unsteadily towards his porthole window.

"Wow!!!!! We really are in the middle of the ocean, it's just beautiful out there and the sea is soooooo calm, so blue, deep, deep blue. Everything seems so peaceful."

Indeed, the contrast was so being out in the middle of the High Seas was certainly different than living in the middle of a great big Metropolis like Hanley. There was not one sound to be heard, only the occasional creaking of the boat. And the salty sea lapping at her boughs as she majestically ploughed through and rode those ocean waves with ease.

JG could not help but stare out of his porthole. He was enchanted by the watery world that surrounded him and, just for a moment, forgot why he was here, and the importance of the journey ahead, he let his mind wander as if he was just going on a boat trip as an adventure, a holiday.

Then reality hit him with a bang as Gabriel entered the room, followed by Jericho, bounding in behind him like a faithful lapdog.

"So, I guess you know that your mum and dad are fine," said Gabriel.

"Hi, Gabriel," answered JG as he turned towards the Wolf Dog. "Yes Lizzie told me, she said you would explain everything."

"And so I will, last night after the Good Tribes People had taken care of the boat. Atohi entered your home, and while your mum and dad were sleeping with much care, he put them under a spell of suspended animation. If I can explain it, it is kind of like putting their lives on hold until you return. That way, they will never know that you have gone. They will remain peacefully asleep and their souls will be free to wander within the safe realms of the Whispering Planes and the Land that Once Was, along with Atohi his people and the Wild Wolves of the West."

"So, you mean, they are free to visit their land?"

"Why of course, once you have been blessed by Atohi, all humans have a kind of free pass to enter his realm."

"However, remember this though, they will be well taken care of, and will be waiting for you as normal when you return home."

"And What a Day that will be!!!!!" JG looked at Gabriel, Gabriel looked back at him, amber eyes aglow, "so let's do it, let's find the Island. Come on team, gather round Lizzie, Jericho, a group hi-five is in order, don't you think?"

The boat sailed on and the friends were prepared, they would do whatever it took to stand together.

Chapter 26

Meanwhile, not so far behind, as predicted under Orbotron's orders, the team of Security Guards aka Galaxy's End were on track and closing in on JG and his team. Orbotron, of course, had taken the reins of the mission and was happy to control his men from the comfort of his lab back at the Silver Oval.

A flock of Vamcreepers were also on board, along with the Ratscorps, these mutants were ready to do battle. They had evil and menace pumping through their veins, Black Knight and Black Sun, of course, were definite ones to look out for as they would stop at nothing to impress Orbotron and secure a forever home on planet earth.

Black Sun already had some suspicions regarding Eddie Eezzie; there was something about him. Something that he sensed and being a rather perceptive creature, he felt that Eddie was not completely under his master's control. He did not act like the other guards. Black Sun was almost 100% sure that Eddie was free from the mind control spell and guessing correctly, he was just playing along until the time was right. He was probably already spying for JG, and JG and his crew would probably be aware that they were being followed by them. This would surely make the Vamcreepers mission more difficult to pull off. Forewarned was forearmed after all. He must watch Eddie like a hawk.

The tracking device was working like a dream, as Orbotron monitored every moment. He had not slept since the boats had set sail and was eager for them to find land soon, in the form of the Long Lost Island.

His plan would then go into overdrive, he would wait patiently for the meeting to take place between JG and Flora (this lady children is an extremely important character in our story) for now though, I will introduce her to you as Nature's Guardian (you will get to know her a lot better very soon).

Orbotron could not help grinning to himself as he played the downfall of Flora over and over again in his mind.

They will bring her to me. They will bring that lovely Lady to me. Imagining the scene Orbotron was working himself into a state of frenzy, the thought of having Flora imprisoned within the walls of the Silver Oval.

"Dooommmed, she will be. Doomed until the end of time. Her secrets will be mine and she will be banished forever. No human alive today or in the future, will never have any knowledge that she ever existed, she will just become like they call it an urban legend."

"And, so be it!" he shrieked, rubbing his spindly hands together as he continued to watch the boats on the sea through the means of his tracking device.

Five days out on the high seas had passed in no time, and they were all settling into their roles on the big waves.

Obviously, the luxury and ease of the boat made her such a pleasure to sail in. At times, they did not even feel like they were on water. And each night, they would sleep peacefully after stargazing and storytelling out on deck.

The morning of the 5th July 2050, 6.00 am, JG and Gabriel sat together in the Control Room, while the rest of the crew was still sleeping.

They both knew that they were being followed and it was quite obvious to them that the evil alien was behind it. By this notion, they were certainly not deterred and were rather calm about the super sleek yacht that was close on their tails, albeit, beautiful she was a symbol of malice and bad intent. Both of them knew that from this point forward, they would have to be high on their guard.

Thank goodness for small mercies, Eddie would not let them down. Between them, they could double cross the Vamcreepers and Ratscorps and collaborate Orbotron's downfall, thus, liberating the rest of the band. This, they were sure of.

What they were not sure of is when they would strike, and when would Orbotron give the 'go ahead' for an attack. Those Vamcreepers were growing more restless by the day, Gabriel could sense this and they along with the Ratscorps were more than ready to wage war on JG and his crew.

JG took comfort in the thought that Atohi would most definitely keep to his promise, and Aranck would be there to join them once they reached the island.

Disturbing JG from his thoughts Gabriel spoke, "I think it would be a good idea to take a look at the Manuscript, I have just been checking and double checking and according to our satellite map and if luck is on our side, we should be pretty close to the Island in approximately one week's time."

"Really, Gabriel? That is Great News!!!!! It will be fantastic to see Aranck again."

"Once we arrive at the island, our first priority is to seek out Flora," said Gabriel.

"Who is Flora?" asked JG inquisitively.

"Well, you may say that this young lady will prove to be the most important link to this whole venture. You will find out soon enough."

"And, yes, we will definitely need Aranck. He knows where to find Flora and will lead us through the Path of Palms and the Rainforest until we reach the Evergreen Glades where Flora resides in a simple Tree House amongst the birds."

"Here, Gabriel, I have the manuscript, just think how old it is, and what wisdom it holds within its binding." JG carefully and with the upmost respect turned the pages until he found the map; this was the very map he had discovered some three years ago when he had first started visiting the library. He was drawn to it then, just like now. But now it seemed more real. Now it had a purpose and had taken on a life force all of its own. The Lost Island of Sacred Souls was almost in his grasp.

Chapter 27

The crew had settled early that evening and as usual sat out on deck, taking in the view, all eyes fixed and gazing out to sea. Lizzie the canary was the first to notice amongst the great swill of the waves shapes that appeared to be horses; magnificent, white horses. It did not take long until the rest of the crew had noticed them.

Gabriel knew at once who these creatures were, and why they had appeared to them almost like a vision. Their bright white hides contrasted with the midnight blue sea, long silver manes flowing outstretched across the water, they were breathtakingly beautiful, and it was a dramatic scene to witness in the middle of the ocean on that calm, calm evening.

The horses started to advance closer to the boat and whinnied to Gabriel, he immediately edged over the side to greet them. JG was curious to find out what was happening, and he, too, edged his way over so that he was in good view of the horses.

"Come, JG," said Gabriel. "Come, let it be my greatest pleasure to introduce you to the Spirits of the Sea. Their appearance signifies that we are closer to the Island than what we had first assumed. Flora has sensed our approach and it is she who has sent her White Horses in peace. So that they can safely escort us to the shores."

"They tell me that they are aware of evil lurking in the shadows. We are to be on our guard against the flock of hell birds and a pack of Ratscorps our enemies. JG, they are close on track, and the Spirits of the Sea senses that an attack is imminent. Therefore, we should put all our energies into navigating the boat swiftly forwards. With their great strength, the horses have the ability to calm the waters. The weather will, from this point onwards, quickly change as a tropical storm is approaching. Take a look ahead. Look at those gigantic waves. There above, look towards the sky, lightning flashes and thunderous clouds are appearing on the horizon. We cannot do battle with nature, but in the same breath, nature has sent us her horses to guide us safely towards the shore."

"All hands on deck!!!" cried out JG at the top of his voice. He quite fancied himself as Captain. He was growing into his sea legs fast. No longer did he feel nauseous. He was truly developing, shall we say, as an old sea birds character.

"Masts down," he called out a second command just as a huge wave came crashing towards them, overflowing the decks. The storm would not wait for them. How quickly the calmness had melted away into the back of yonder, as the full force of the storm was quickly upon them.

As its full strength quickly became apparent, Gabriel lunged into action working with the Spirits of the Sea, who by now were more than ready to part the waves to ensure safe access to the shores beyond.

Gabriel navigated by pure intuition, as JG left the decks above and quickly resumed his position in the control room. He intently watched the satellite display which was programmed to guide the sailing boat's every move. Dad had cleverly installed a special device for storms such as these. *Sometimes Dad is just too clever!* JG thought to himself. "Good one Dad," he said out loud. "You may have just got us through with your sneaky little invention."

Nature sure was whipping up one beast of a storm, perhaps she was challenging him, JG thought. She may even be testing my courage, she wants me to prove to her that I am ready, ready to fight for Planet Earth and gain respect from the Great Flora.

Jericho and Lizzie looked in amazement as the Spirits of the Sea gracefully worked together to part the waves, "What strength! What power!" commented Jericho. The Husky could not believe her eyes. She turned her attentions towards Gabriel, as he bravely stood on deck working with the horses. She knew then she had found her soul mate.

Back in the control room, things had started to get a little sparky!!! A little less calm. A lot of bother was brewing in the shape and form of yes, you may have guessed it, the sworn enemy Orbotron. There had been reports that his sleek yacht was edging ever closer. Since the two boats set sail some two weeks ago, the enemy has been following his tracking device day and night. Sleeping rarely, of course, he could not miss a single report of the progress across the seas. The cunning alien knows every move, every inch of JG's progress. He knows about the Sprits of the Sea and their rescue plan, he knows about the parting of the waves, and he simply must stay on track and seize his chance to lunge his yacht forward while there is a path. If he loses JG now, it could cost him dearly.

With fury and determination in his cold, wicked, heart, Orbotron communicates his thoughts to his team of security guards. Eddie Eezzie has also been assigned to the control room, and has been following the satellite while battling pounding rain; waves as big as houses and thunderous lightning struck sky.

It must be said that the poor guy is struggling, the sleek yacht for all her technology and power, will just not ride these waves. Eddie is blinded by a fit of panic; just for a second in time, his vision is lost. It returns just in time to focus on the cruel sea thrashing out uncontrollable waves, lightning strikes once again across the wicked sky, like you have never seen in your life. It strikes once, it strikes twice, it strikes three times and for a fateful moment, it feels like the end of the world. The storm has come to take them all away, and away it will, if Eddie does not get a grip.

It may not be the right moment but Rock Music has always been Eddie's salvation, he knows he must keep up with JG so they can overthrow Orbotron together.

So what does he do??? To pull him through??? He starts creating a new song. Now children, you might want to ask yourselves this is no time for song creation but when it comes to Eddie, as we all know by now, this chappie likes living a little bit on the edge, shall we say. All this drama and high natural energy produced by the storm, who needs a music studio, the atmosphere is just perfect for song writing, and write he does. He gets the groove and the notion, and the words just flow. It's a pity he does not have his guitar, he could string out the tune, no problem. As he reaches a high note, the great sleek yacht suddenly leaps out of the water and crashes into a humongous wave a dramatic ending as *Storm Seekers Symphony* (this being the title of his new track) is thus created in Eddie's mind. He is on stage with his band playing to an adoring crowd of 10,000 people.

Back on board JG's sailing boat, things are starting to calm down a little. Thank Goodness, the passage through the ocean has been created and all that is left for JG's teammates to do now is to keep focused and follow the Spirits of the Sea, the Great Flora awaits her protégé.

Chapter 28

"Wow!!!!! How those horses can move!" exclaimed JG, as he returned on deck to find Gabriel.

"They are not called the Spirits of the Sea for nothing, you know," commented Gabriel.

"You did well, mate, up here out on deck throughout all the chaos. You really held it together, Gabriel, I would be truly lost without you."

As the horses continued, the sailing boat picked up speed and they were making excellent progress. "I estimate another three days journey and we will be there," said Gabriel.

"Then the adventure really begins," remarked JG. "We are certainly ready for it."

Eddie and his crew had also made it through the storm, although, it was a different story on their yacht. Nowhere near as peaceful. There was no rejoicing as each night these poor guys had to put up with the endless cawing and eerie sounds made by the hell birds, the Vamcreepers. By now they were desperate to reach land, to spread their vampire-like wings and create a reign of terror, striking fear into their enemies, so they hoped.

As for the other mutants on board, the fiendish Ratscorps, they were ready too! And had gnawed and nibbled their way through a whole ten feet long crate of garbage mix. This disgusting substance had begun to produce a pungent smell that was steadily rising upwards to the decks. Eddie and the crew had constant blinding headaches caused by both groups of mutant creatures. Not to mention Orbotron's relentless commands, demands and instructions, which would telepathically be transformed into their brains. It was fast becoming a living nightmare for these poor guys, and Eddie could not see the time of day until they docked. With priority number one, to find JG and join forces, he certainly could not wait to release the shackles that Orbotron had objected them to.

"Revenge is sweet," said Eddie, smiling to himself, "revenge will sure be sweet," as he stepped out onto the top deck to examine the ocean. He cried out these words at the top of his voice, somewhere in that vast expanse of water JG may have heard him, who knows?????

Finally, some three days later, Land Ahoy was on the horizon. It was 12th July 2050. "Halleluliah!!!!!"

"Let's hear it, guys. Altogether now, Halleuluiah!!!!! Our Island Destination lies straight ahead," as the sprawling mass of land became visibly apparent.

"Wow!!!!! What a sight she was." JG recognised where they were without hesitation. He had seen it over and over again inside the manuscript. In real life, however, The Island of Sacred Souls took your breath away. The force and the power which it emulated, was so apparent it could be felt some five miles out at sea.

Green, emerald green, with sand as white as snowfall and waters as blue and deep as an exotic priceless sapphire. The Island could only be described as an out and out winner within the stereotypical, super exclusive holiday destinations but without all mod cons and minus the demanding, spoilt tourists.

"You know, Gabriel my friend, I could sit out here on deck and gawk at the Island all day."

"I know exactly what you mean JG, but stop daydreaming, or maybe should I say really make the most of your daydream as this is the calm before the storm. You need to be sharp and ready for action as soon as we pull into that bay over there."

The horses had started to slow down, no longer did they gallop at maximum horsepower speed. Now they had pulled into a soft canter. As they whinnied and pranced about in the relaxed waves, they were clearly enjoying themselves. They had triumphed above the storm, and Flora would be most content with their work of safely delivering her special guests.

There was just one problem which was manifesting in Neve's sharp mind. She knew that the enemies were close on track, she could sense them and was determined to inform Flora immediately. Although Flora had been expecting this invasion for some time, and being her intuitive self would probably already know her enemies were at large, and closing in on them fast.

Surely, they could not lose this conflict against Orbotron and his cursed mutants. Flora would be confident of success, the people and the wolves from the Land that Once Was and the Whispering Planes would most definitely help them win this looming, inevitable and epic battle.

Calmly, JG and his loyal crew followed the horses into the sheltered bay. The horses could finally rest a while. As the herd left the sea, JG noticed that every muscle was visible through their white hides.

JG remembered Gabriel's advice and was as alert as an eagle as he scanned the landscape searching for any indication that Aranck had arrived. After searching for some time, JG began to wonder whether he had dreamt all that had happened previously in the Land That Once Was, maybe his friendship with Aranck had just been a figment of his imagination. And then, JG with much relief spotted him in the distance, Aranck was staring right at him lounged across a large boulder, and looking very much at home. A Mountain Loin as bold as bold could be, Aranck had wisely chosen his animal form. The Good Tribes People were true to their word; JG could not contain his excitement as he made his way swiftly in the direction to greet Aranck. As he picked up pace, he remembered the teachings of the Tribes People on the fine art of shape shifting, he could feel his animal emerging underneath his skin. Leaping into his animal form, the Puma, he could run. *This sure is impressive stuff,* he thought to himself, and within seconds JG was face to face with the Bold Mountain Lion. The two big cats stood there staring at one another showing mutual respect. They were clearly happy to be in one another's company once again.

"It's fantastic that you made it, Aranck. I have really missed you."

"And I you, my friend. You did well to remember our teachings. You look quite the big cat in your Puma skin."

"Thanks, Aranck. Yes, I am rather proud of him, he is just such a coooooool character."

"OK, now greetings over with, let us get down to business," suggested Aranck with a big smile on his face.

“As you are probably aware JG, time is of the essence, we have been sent word that Orbotron’s yacht complete with his security guards and mutant creatures are nearing the island. Yes, they made it through the storm and if our senses are accurate, they will be here by nightfall. This gives us exactly 10 hours of daylight to prepare ourselves. We, immediately, must make the journey to Flora. She is waiting for us in her tree top canopy, high in the middle of those mountains,” Aranck indicated to a lush green mountain range far in the distance.

“I suggest that you round up your crew, and we should get going while the day is on our side. In fact the weather is perfect for our assent, there is a cool breeze coming in from the sea, and the sun is shining. Who could ask for more? Let’s go!!!”

Chapter 29

Within minutes the journey had commenced, Aranck took the lead followed by Neve, and her faithful herd. Spirits were high amongst them. They kept good pace. JG was eager to meet the Great Flora, and the thought of this really spurred him on.

Gabriel and Jericho had grown really close over these last two weeks, Jericho was learning fast from her new friend. She had become more intuitive, you could say. He brought the Wolf out in her. Lizzie, the white canary, felt safe perched high on JG's shoulder. She was his look out small but very effective when it came to spotting even the smallest of details.

That day they were carried away by the cool breeze, coming in from the sea and at the same time bathed by the warm sunshine. This band of courageous characters could have put any marathon runners to shame. As they journeyed forthwith, JG felt so alive again. He was a true Puma meandering through the undergrowth of the jungle.

They must have been travelling for some time when Aranck started to slow down. They neared a plateau, shaded by a group of tall palm trees. He pulled up ranks and suggested that they rested for a while, he estimated that they would safely reach Flora's canopy in approximately two hours.

Looking up towards the magnificent mountain range, JG could only imagine how Flora would be. He thought she must be some brave lady to live out here all alone in this paradise. Wilderness appeared so perfectly to him, it almost did not seem real. As if he was a character playing a role in a story tale, he gazed down at his huge paws and felt very comfortable in his animal skin.

It was Aranck who broke the silence and brought JG out of his daydream. "Ahum. Ahum. No!!! No!!! No, JG. This will not do, this will not do at all, daydreaming on the job. Roar, Roar," he joked as he played around with his vocals.

"Hey! Aranck. Sorry, man." The two great cats stood side by side and gazed upwards towards the mountains. "You ought to teach me how to roar like that one day. It would certainly add a bit of kick to my Puma and would definitely complete the Big Cat profile."

"Well, today is your lucky day, JG. We have about five minutes before we set off again. I suppose I can teach you.

"First, close your eyes. Just listen to your body, listen to your surroundings. Feel your Puma's heart beating hard inside your chest. Now keep with the rhythm, imagine that you are out there in that tropical wilderness, your stalking your prey, you are on a mission and you need to eat today. Open up your mind to the sounds around you. Feel the power of the wilderness; breathe in the aromas, the bare earth, the woodiness of the trees, the scents of the flowers. Are you with me????? Can you feel it?????

"If the answer is yes and if you have connected with your Puma from the bottom of your heart, just go with it. Now open your eyes and roar like you mean business."

"Roar, and roar again."

"Wow!!!" feeling it was an understatement, JG roared right on cue as the echo of his powerful sounds resonated around the plateau.

"Good Job, good job, my friend. Well, I think you have got it. With passion like that, I don't think we will have much problem in defeating Orbotron and his mutant crew." That sudden thought brought JG right back down to earth and filled his heart with dread. Amongst all this beauty, a potent battle would soon be taking place.

Neve approached them with a soft whiney. Aranck instantly knew what she wanted, it was time to leave this point onwards, the white horse would take the lead. Only she and she alone knew the way through the Path of Palms onwards and upwards which would eventually lead to the Tree Top Canopy home of the Great Flora.

Silver manes and swishing tales took to the undergrowth, this rugged path proved to throw some obstacles in the way of our intrepid warriors, but they soon got the hang of it. Well, they simply had no choice, if they wanted to keep up with the spirited, white horses.

In some parts the road was treacherous, and you could say, their dear lives were hanging in the balance. But those horses just would not slow down. They cleared every sharp corner, twist or bend with ease. They did not skim one single rock. Unlike JG and the others, they were skimming rocks left, right and centre.

"Don't look down," cried out Aranck. "Guys, whatever you do, do not look down," as they approached a spiral like formation jutting out of the rock. "Just to give you all a huge injection of confidence at this most precarious time, the spiral you see ahead of you signifies the end of this rocky assent. Soon we will reach the smooth lanes, which are famously known as the Path of Palms. In other words, what I am trying to say to you guys is: literally hold onto your horses. We are going up to go smooth."

"Could Flora not have found an easier place to live?????" joked JG.

"Now, that would make it too easy," remarked Gabriel, his wolf side was just kicking in as they embarked on the spiral path. Jericho looked on and bravely followed her soul mate Gabriel, she knew she was safe as long as he was around. There is just no fooling a wise, young wolf.

After a few near misses, at last and thank goodness for small mercies, the group had reached the tallest peak of the spiral rock formation. Much relief was felt by all to finally reach the smooth planes.

This beautiful landscape could be described as rather like a long sandy beach; high up in the mountains, boarded on either side by lustrous green gigantic Palm Trees, the sand underfoot felt like soft golden velvet and after the pounding rocks, it was certainly comforting under foot. To add to its glory, it was warm too!!! Just the right temperature.

On the horizon, you could just make out Flora's tree top canopy nestled in the tropical distance. Even from far away, a feeling of peace resonated towards them. Neve and the herd were overjoyed to be returning back home, they pranced and tossed their heads, displaying their beautiful silver manes in a proud dance of joy.

"Well, JG. What do you think? How do you feel to be so close to Flora? The landscape is amazing, is it not?"

“At this moment Aranck, I am without words, to be honest though, I am starting to feel a little nervous, as I am not quite sure what to expect.”

“Just chill, JG, think deep thoughts. Enjoy this soft sand underfoot, or should I say, under paw.”

“HA-HA! That’s a point, don’t you think? I should meet Flora in my human form?”

“As you wish, JG. I will change back too if it makes you feel better? So for now, let’s say goodbye to our big cats to be returned to at a later date.”

“Woohoo! Well, look at you. Hey man, your hair has grown. In fact, you have grown, and yes, you seem to have gotten a little more, shall we say, muscular around those shoulders.”

“Well, we could put that down to the last nine hours of rock climbing,” answered JG. “Hey, got one for you. If you fancy a crash course in extreme rock climbing contact Aranck, from the Whispering Planes on the following number: 3312452421.”

“I am hoping to achieve a 6 pack to complete the look,” JG half-joked back (but between you and me young readers, he would probably be quite happy with a six-pack), “When can I hire you for an extreme exercise regime in gaining some first class abs?” JG continued.

“OK, can I just say my schedule, unfortunately, is pretty tight right at the moment. Plus, don’t we have an alien to exterminate? Look me up in a few weeks, when things have quietened down a little but on one condition,” said Aranck.

“What is that?” enquired JG.

“The very next time you arrange a festival, you will invite me, OK?”

“Consider it a done deal,” said JG, the two friends looked at one another and instantly knew that they could trust each other and would always keep to their promises. Jokes and much laughter made up a big part of their relationship. JG smiled to himself and thought Aranck was so easy to hang out with, he was so wise, given the cultural background that he had, descending from the Goods Tribes People. But he was also tuned in to the modern world and could switch easily between the two. JG just loved the fact that he could pick up on all his humorous ways.

Chapter 30

After all the banter and joking around, time had quickly passed, Neve and her herd signalled a sharp stop as they pulled up into a shady clearing bursting with the most amazing plants, trees and tropical flowers. This was obviously Flora's garden and standing right in front of them was the famous Tree Top Canopy, Flora's home.

Above the roof, a flock of paradise birds circled above its peaks. They looked friendly enough; they certainly were colourful, blessed with an elaborate plumage and melodious tones, suspiciously keeping their eyes on JG and his group. They had Flora's best interest at heart and were obviously her look outs. Neve whinnied something to them and they seemed to settle down.

Suddenly the tree house doors were flung wide open, and there she was in all her glory, Flora. The first thing JG noticed about her was her smile, then her eyes and then he realised how young she was. JG had imagined a woman, but this being was just a girl and younger than him, he was guessing around 11/12, and then she spoke.

"Yes, you are correct," she smiled, "I am 11 years old." JG was in shock, she had just read his mind, his thoughts. He remained confused, as she gracefully made her way down the cleverly crafted rope ladder to greet her excited and awe stricken guests.

"Welcome, my friends," she proceeded, dressed simply in a pair of roughly cut bleached denim shorts and a white lace blouse. She had tanned olive skin and long flowing, shiny brown hair, her eyes were as dark and smooth as chocolate.

Flora could have been just your regular pretty, eleven year old girl, but no, there was something deeply special about her. It was so much more than just good looks, this was strongly apparent at first contact.

Gabriel instinctively lay down by her feet like a big soft teddy bear. She gazed down at him and stroked his head, on doing so, his wise amber eyes seemed to glow the deepest of yellow as he clearly enjoyed her touch.

"Can I just say, it is wonderful to have you all here, I have been waiting for you for some time, you know!"

"Come, you must all be tired and in need of some refreshments," she beckoned the group to follow her as she led them to a long wooden table and chairs underneath the shade of two large palm trees. The day was really quite hot and they were relieved to be out of the sun as they sat back and relaxed after their journey. They really felt that a good rest was definitely in order. Flora was proving to be a wonderful host as she proceeded to pour them all a refreshing drink.

"Wow! This is good stuff!" Aranck exclaimed.

"I am glad you like it," said Flora. "It is my own recipe made from Coconut Milk, ice and the freshest of lemons with a hint of sugar."

"So thirst quenching," said JG, as he sat back and gazed up at the blue sky glinting through the giant palm trees, they had truly found paradise. They were going to enjoy it for a little while anyway, before all hell breaks loose.

To tempt her guests further, Flora had also prepared to serve food which was set to get their appetites flowing. There were salad bowls with all kinds of different salad leaves JG had never seen before in his life, delicious smelling fresh bread, baked buns and loaves, grilled fish and seafood, obviously, fresh from the lagoons and the surrounding ocean, there were some mouth-watering fruits. Yes, you have guessed it, all tropical pineapples, bananas, mangos, papayas, even oranges, apples and strawberries were amongst them. There were even some handmade chocolates for afters, which looked just delicious. Yes, Flora had gone all out to look after them, this girl seemed to be able to make something out of nothing.

Under the protective palm trees, they ate and drank with gusto. Flora felt happy that her guests were enjoying the picnic she had lovingly prepared for them.

Away from the happy scene, trouble was brewing. Flora could sense it as her happy heart sunk under the threatening doom. Obviously, she did not want to alarm her relaxing guests. Sleep was what they needed now and as they were coming to the end of their feast, Flora unbeknown to them commenced a soft soothing chant, accompanied by Sky, one of the birds of paradise. Well as you can imagine, the chant did the trick. Within moments, the group were all sleeping peacefully.

Gabriel, although, did not fall asleep. Flora and him went back a long way and were old friends, you could say. They had met through realms of time and crossings of worlds, as the forces of Earth's Guardians, often did.

They crept away from beneath the trees and it was Flora who spoke first. "The chosen boy is just as I had imagined him to be. You have taught him well, Gabriel."

"Oh, thank you, my dear Flora. I will take that as a compliment. I am glad you approve. He is determined to face Orbotron and help the planet recover and replenish itself, after we have rid ourselves of our alien invader."

"Speaking of Orbotron!" exclaimed Flora. "My island friends have informed me that his yacht is due to dock anytime now. So from this point onwards, time is precious we have much planning to do. We just have to be successful in this battle or we are set to lose everything."

Now children you may be thinking if the evil Orbotron is going to challenge JG and his friends in person, will he cross the ocean to the Lost Island of Sacred Souls? Will he be prepared to fight for what he wants? Or will he remain in the confines of his silver Oval? While his mutants and hypnotised security guards commence his dirty work and carry out his evil plan, all will be revealed soon enough.

Chapter 31

Now children, if you please, let me take you back to the Financial District in the City of Hanley. Destination – the Silver Oval, of course! Now, let's go inside and creep down deep into its vaults. Here we will find Orbotron who has not slept for almost two weeks. Still sat connected to his computer system, scrupulously checking his tracking device for any signs of the yacht's landing. And then he noticed the good news, his smooth yacht had finally docked.

"Oh, yes! Yes!" he bellows, "They have finally docked." The vaults immediately shook with Orbotron's high-pitched sounds of delight at his conquest. "Flora, my dear, much dread you must fear. No vast ocean, no beast of a storm, no untouchable manuscript can keep me away from your shores. Mark my words, I am coming for you!!!!!" he shrieked, an out of this world shriek that no human being or animal was capable of emulating, it was pure alien vocals of the creepiest kind.

Back on the Island of Sacred Souls, Flora felt a shudder down her spine, as the wrath of Orbotron engulfed her frame, like a black cloak covering the sun. And outside, a sharp misty chill touched the Path of Palms and just for a second, the endless blue sky turned a murky grey.

"Gabriel, I fear to admit this but our alien friend has one powerful touch, let's just say I certainly know what kind of energy we are dealing with here."

"I can fully appreciate that!" exclaimed Gabriel.

Orbotron continued to look at his screen. His soulless, black eyes fixated on what was unfolding before him, he could make out the security guards led by Eddie disembarking from the yacht. Then he saw his faithful Vamcreepers led by Black Sun and Black Knight, the flock of terror birds were efficiently and swiftly falling into flock order, soon to come onto the scene. Not to forget the monstrous Ratscorps, who after two weeks at sea, cooped up in their huts had grown fat and cumbersome after binging continuously on their foul garbage. Unlike the precise Vamcreepers, they struggled to get into line as they fought and grumbled at one another, displaying their long yellow teeth and crooked claws. These guys definitely looked menacing and in sharp contrast to the beautiful, paradise landscape. They looked totally out of place here. Anyone who had the displeasure to meet them that evening would surely wish to banish them back to their squalid sewers forever.

Orbotron took a deep breath as he pondered over the scene on the beach. His spindly fingers outstretched and poised at the controls. Yes, they had made it to the island, yes, they were on their way to seek out JG and Flora, but something was not quite right here. Orbotron had a niggle, as he tapped away at the control panel, his bony white fingers danced around while his crooked mind worked overtime.

"That's it, that's it!!!!!" he shrieked as only an alien could do with those vocal chords. "It's that Eddie fellow, I always knew there was something about him, UM!!! Bad judgement on my side, bad judgement indeed, he certainly is one strong human to crack, I must admit my ego this time has got the better of me."

"A mere human has been strong enough to break my curse, all the while he has been playing with me, stringing me along, making me believe that he was still under my spell."

"Well, there is only one thing for it. I will have to go and do my own dirty work. In fact, I will quite enjoy crushing those miserable beings myself. Let the Games begin."

Orbotron could travel light. All he needed was his brainpower and his tracking device; he was ready for action and action. He would cause as he elevated out from his beloved vaults, spiralling upwards in a shroud of grey toxic mist. Destination – The Island of Sacred Souls.

Back on the Island, Flora felt that dread once again and knew instantly that things had taken a turn for the worse. Orbotron was on his way in person.

"Gabriel!" Flora exclaimed, "I hate to tell you this but Orbotron has left the vaults. He is making his way across the ocean to take matters into his own hands. It looks like we will have to face him after all. And what is strange is, is my mind is blocked by thoughts of him. He has somehow locked into my psyche, I can feel it, he is trying to weaken me; to absorb my thoughts and secrets of the island and the life of a Nature Guardian, his desire to own the manuscript is also his intention. I must resort to the skill of meditation which will help me build a force against him, and rise above his control, I can't play his mind games when our world is at stake," she proceeded to perform a chant, stepping outside her tree house. She made her way across the sandy path to a natural spring of water and knelt down beside it to begin her enchantment.

Gabriel's thoughts quickly turned to JG and the others. He would have to awaken them soon from their deep slumber. At sunrise tomorrow, they would have to be ready to face the enemy.

Whether it was the idea of Orbotron making his way across that vast ocean that chilled the night or was it just a figment of their imaginations, something out there had certainly interfered with the warm evenings this island usually enjoyed. Looking out to sea, a murky mist was taking form and was, without doubt, visible along the horizon. Orbotron's toxic curse had started to manifest itself and permeate the pure atmosphere of the Lost Island of Sacred Souls.

For the Vamcreepers, who were making good progress towards the mountain range which would lead them to the Path of Palms, the toxic atmosphere was like an energy rush. They immediately absorbed it into their lungs revelling in the power it gave them, likewise, for the hideous Ratscorps who also took full advantage of this potent soup.

But our poor security guards aka Galaxy's End had started to suffer and show signs of strain as they tried to cope under these fast becoming unbearable polluted conditions. The gases burned their eyes and noses. They were finding it hard to see through the grey gloom.

Eddie was no fool. He soon recognised a swift change in how the mutant creatures benefitted from this polluted mass that had by now, totally changed the pure atmosphere. How could something happen so quickly? Eddie soon realised that Orbotron would definitely have something to do with this. And if he had guessed correctly, was probably on his way to join his mutant crew.

Eddie had always despised the Vamcreepers and the Ratscorps, that shared our world, but after spending two whole weeks with them on the yacht in the middle of the ocean, his hatred had grown with every passing day. *Yuk, err! Mutants,* were his thoughts as he watched the two armies thriving and determined to carry out their quest. Orbotron had certainly made it clear to them that they must defeat JG and Flora.

So to cheer himself up a bit and to keep his mind focused and positive, what did Eddie do? Yes, he thought of music. Music was his saviour, and he started humming the first few words of a tune with the words Toxic Mutants. He yelled at the top of his voice, chuckling to himself as he envisaged his guitar and playing once again to his many fans. Soon enough, his thoughts swiftly changed. "Come on, man," he said to himself, "snap out of your day dream, this is serious stuff now. JG needs me as he set his mind on a clear-cut victory."

We will return now young readers to the Path of Palms., Dawn is fast approaching and JG is about to awake from his slumber. During the night, he had risen in and out of sleep, thoughts of home of his mum and dad, visions of the Whispering Planes, The Good Tribes People, The Wise Wild Wolves of the West had come together in his dreams to wish him well and to bless him courage and strength. All that he had learnt during the past few months, now, seemed to have fallen into place and a wave of confidence replenished his soul.

At daybreak, it was clearly apparent that the island had been cursed with the toxic mist. It had viciously spread during the night and had now engulfed the Path of Palms. That morning, sadly, there were no sunny, bright sky, no cheerful bird song, no sounds at all from the animal kingdom. All was silent, a grey mist loomed and lingered through the giant palms. The sun's life giving rays had been blocked out by Orbotron's deadly concoction, and that evil fiend was less than half an hour away from the sacred island's shoreline.

On another note to make matters worse, the mutants had just reached the spiral pathway in the rock formation, and were eager to make their assent, as they felt even stronger after a nights feed on the toxic matter and the polluted atmosphere. This could not be said for our friend Eddie and his band, who were under more strain than ever, and were totally unprepared and exhausted as they looked up at the steep mountain path which, obviously, they must now begin to climb. The Vamcreepers were keeping their beady eyes on the bedraggled men. Eddie and his crew looked petrified. Eddie tried to sound chirpy, "OK guys, are you with me??? A big heave-ho and we are on our way."

"Eddie man, have you seen the height of that thing?" shouted out Lex Lizard, "you are seriously telling me we have to climb that."

"I am afraid so, Lex. Just trust me, OK? Keep the faith. I will go first. I will be the guinea pig. Come on, it might not be that bad, once we get going."

Eddie was wrecked with doubt but he had to keep it together. Even though the rest of the band was still under Orbotron's hypnotic spell, they still were capable of their own thoughts, now and then. They must get to JG to help him defeat the alien. Upon looking up, he could see the Vamcreepers closely followed by the Ratscorps they already were making good progress. This was easy for them.

Led by Black Sun and Black Knight, who were both eager to impress their master. Unbeknown to anyone else, a private battle was being played out between the two. Vamcreepers as they both strived to be the best.

Back at the Path of Palms, it wasn't long before the first hellish Vamcreeper Black Sun, made his shocking appearance. The very sight of his vast wingspan and his long sharp talons were threatening enough, let alone the dreadful cawing sound, which he continued to make, obviously, trying to intimidate his enemies.

It was Sky, one of the paradise island birds, who first noticed him as he certainly made no secret about his presence. He was here for a reason, he was here to win, and just the mere sight of him soaring in and out of the Palms was enough to chill your soul, he was calling for others to join him and soon enough, they would arrived, followed by hordes of long toothed scorpion tailed, Ratscorps,

JG and his companions gathered themselves under the canopy. As they peered upwards they could clearly see that the sun was completely blocked, the scene was such laid out before your eyes, a few moments of solace of comradeship, a time to stand together to concentrate on justice and victory. This beautiful vision of love and friendship was a sharp contrast to the eerie, relentless calling of the approaching Vamcreepers.

Flora asked them all to keep calm, if at all possible, as once again she began her meditation; an enchantment of deep, deep power that was born from this sacred land, the white herd. The Spirits of the Sea led by Neve cantered into the clearing, proud as ever, their magnificent necks arched, manes a flowing scraping at the earth with their poised hooves. They were ready to battle.

My friends exclaimed Flora as she still carried out her enchantment with eyes closed, she asked them all to focus on the island, the sea, the mountains, the beaches and lagoons, the plants, rivers and streams, the diversity of the animal and sea life kingdom. The colours and beauty with which they paint our world. Without this gift, life would have little purpose, and we would surely lose everything to a grey toxic world. Now known as Orbotron's dream.

Suddenly, the enchantment was broken as Flora was approached by a bird of paradise frantically flapping her wings. She had grave news; Orbotron had arrived and he was making his way using his levitation skills, up the spiral rock formation with ease.

Friends called out Aranck in a proud honourable voice as he touched his chest. The moment that we have all been waiting for has finally arrived, "May I take this opportunity to wish each and every one of you well. I hold you all so dear, keep the faith and we will succeed!!!!!"

After relaying his speech of encouragement, Aranck gave the cue to JG which could only mean one thing; their animal forms were to be called upon. Once again, yes, they must shape shift back into their Great Cat roles; Puma and Mountain Lion, who else. With these two noble beasts on board, they were confident and at the same time, a little excited to show one particular alien who is boss.

In less than a second, the two great cats stood shoulder to shoulder in all their glory, and in perfect unison they both let out one mighty roar, which was enough to send threatening shock waves around the Path of Palms and, for a while, it certainly halted and got the attention of the Vamcreepers who had ceased their horrific cawing.

Then another dramatic change, from cawing to roaring, this presence crept into the clearing but this time is was dead silence, followed by dread and doom. It was like time had stood still, nothing, not a sound. Orbotron had darkened the day to the blackest of black as he stood at the foot of the tree house canopy, shrouded by his legions of Vamcreepers and a mass of wriggling red-bellied Ratscorps.

If ever there was a scene from one of your worst nightmares, this one was definitely up for the running.

"Flora, my dear, we meet at last," Orbotron proceeded to speak as he rubbed his spindly white fingers together. "Silence," he shrieked at the excited Ratscorps, who could not contain themselves any longer. The foul creatures were everywhere like a plague from hell.

"UM. UM," he continued taking his usual stance levitating some three feet above the ground. His ever-present cape flowing in the breeze behind him, it almost covered his whole spindly body, apart from his large pulsating head. Indicating as he spoke, he fixated his gaze on Flora, and just for a second she stared back into those bottomless pits (namely his eyes). She almost felt the very heart and soul of her being, being forced out of her body, which sent shockwaves down her spine. She had to break the gaze, "Look away now, look away nowwwww!" she told herself. "Friends," she warned, "whatever you do, do not look into his eyes, they spell evil."

"Strong, am I not?" he spoke. "Don't deny you can't feel my energy field. I, the great Orbotron, have the power and hypnotic skills to take control of your minds. Do you not know the story of our famous little band, Galaxy's End, and how they fell under my most marvellous spell. I am invincible. Let's just say, those guys were lucky enough to meet me. They have a lifelong career now trapped and forever indebted to me."

"You speak with too much confidence, Orbotron. Yes, we can admit you have come this far. You have almost colonised earth, bringing with you, your deadly mist and toxic gases, your concrete and steel, but you have forgotten one thing, friendship and love are stronger than steel and toxic air."

"Fools, you truly believe in all that, do you? That is stuff of fairy tales and dreams. I will show you the right way to live, I will show you the nightmare when you all fallen captive to my master plan. HA – HA – HA – HA," what an evil laugh, was there no stopping this ghastly fiend from worlds beyond?????

Orbotron continued with his demands, "Centuries have passed seeking out your island paradise but sadly to no avail. The years I have spent trying to track down the Manuscript you hold so dear but once again, sadly, to no avail. I could congratulate you on this, if I was feeling kind, but no, Orbotron could not belittle himself with one of your so-called human emotions. Oh no, no, no, that would not do at all. So, what remains to be said? Any one care to hazard a guess?" Orbotron scanned the group for an answer.

Aranck bravely stepped forward, "We just want things to be how they were before a certain intruder came on the scene, and we have the forces and spirit to heal all wrongs and put things right."

"Ah, simplicity in its strongest form. Hey!!! How easy you make it sound. Anyway, enough of this talk. We are getting nowhere." He levitated a foot higher and raised his arms and eyes towards the death sky, summoning his Vamcreepers even closer. With a quick glance down, an evil look on his usually expressionless face became creepily apparent. "So, my dear flora, what happens next?"

Chapter 32

There was a long pause as our brave heroes and their enemy just stared intently at one another. Then Orbotron gave the command as he reached up even higher towards the sky, with his long thin neck and arms his mutants had been telepathically programmed to commence the attack, and attack they did, these grotesque beings needed no further encouragement. Once again led by Black Sun and Black Knight, the ferocious birds swooped down on the unsuspecting group below the Ratscorps. Ready for action, they commenced their attack, their scorpion razor edged tails searching for a victim to maim and slay ultimately to bring Orbotron the victory he so demanded. They were ruthless in their plan to capture Flora and the alien was determined to wipe out all her supporters including JG. At this point the alien realised that Galaxy's End had served their purpose, Eddie Eezzie was clearly no longer under his spell. *And, well the others*, he thought, *let's face it, they are practically useless*, he smirked to himself. *I will do away with them, let's add some more victims to the day.*

Witnessing that fateful scene, it is true to say young readers, that it was one of deep despair. It appeared that the alien was winning the battle as those mutants just kept on coming, there were too many of them and they were relentless in their deadly deed.

Only a miracle could save our heroes now, and thankfully that miracle would come in the form of Atohi, the Good Tribes People, and our old friends, the Wise Wild Wolves of the West.

JG and Aranck in their big cat forms bravely fought on, Gabriel and Jericho's joint strength and courage was a sheer spectacle; they showed no fear as they leaped and bounded though the swarms of Ratscorps, The mist was making it more and more difficult to see, and the oxygen levels by now were extremely low.

Flora and the horses were as swift and agile as cheetahs as they meandered through the swooping flocks of Vamcreepers who had stepped up their game. Let me tell you, ferocious being an understatement, they were programmed to fight until the bitter end and they were taking no prisoners only one live one, which would be Flora.

JG had swiftly learnt how to merge as one with his big cat form. All that Aranck had taught him was paying off. As he battled on, he aimed his great powerful paws at two large hell birds that were getting just a little bit too close for comfort. These things were practically ready to claw his eyes out; he had to think fast, he now found himself cornered. Another five great Vams swooped in to launch their attack, JG was in trouble, "No, it can't end here," he found himself thinking as the Vams proceeded with their vicious attack towards him.

Then revelation came in the form of the amulet, the precious stone which had been gifted to JG by Atohi some months prior. With this knowledge, he found some new strength within himself as his puma form started to fight back with courage and honour. The more he fought off his enemies, the more the warmth and the power grew from the amulet close to his chest. It filled him with wisdom and hope. The precious stone continued to glow the deepest of blue, the exact blue of the river from the Whispering Planes from where the amulet was produced.

Then from the amulet's blue glow, words were projected into the murky sky, illuminating the scene with the ancient inscription; Wan Takun Winhu – May The Great Spirit Walk With You. A swarm of fireflies magically appeared. And then he saw them advancing forwards through the gloom, the Wise Wild Wolves of the West closely followed by Atohi and the Good Tribes People.

JG was filled and thrilled with relief. Through all the confusion, he looked around for Aranck, and when he spotted him victory was written all over his proud Mountain Lion's face. It was only a matter of time now, the end of the alien and his cursed mutant population was nigh.

Without losing any time, Atohi launched himself into the battle with his great staff in hand. He swiftly floored to the ground any mutant that dared throw themselves at him. He frantically searched for Flora who was under attack by Black Sun, who had her held down by her hair. Black Sun had proudly signalled Orbotron and was so pleased of his achievement. The Great Flora was now surely doomed and soon to be Orbotron's prisoner for all eternity.

Neve like Flora was also suffering some cruel wounds as three Ratscorps and a particularly vicious, young Vamp was clawing and pecking at her beautiful white hide; with her nostrils flared open and her hooves pawing the ground with contempt, this beautiful horse would not surrender herself to these brutes, as she bravely reared up and kicked out in pure defiance. Atohi rushed to her defence and leapt onto her back, together they made a good team and soon brought these creatures to a bitter end.

Neve gave the listless Vamp one last hoofing and its body turned to dust. This was becoming quickly apparent across the battlefield as each slain mutant turned to dust, leaving no remains behind of its past being.

The battle wore on, the Wise Wild Wolves of the West had victoriously brought down a flock of over five hundred Vams, they were no match for our faithful friends. These Wolves were true stealth hunters and they did not like to fail. To see them in action was to see teamwork at its best.

Chapter 33

Meanwhile, Flora who had now escaped form the evil clutches of Black Sun, thanks to Atohi and the wolves, was fighting her own private battle with Orbotron. He had cunningly followed her to the clearing which lead to the woods. He had sensed that his plan was failing as Flora had broken free, and out of his clutches, his mutants were being slain and turning to dust left right and centre. The wolves and the Good Tribes People were proving to be a force to be reckoned with, and Orbotron was feeling very nervous, very nervous indeed. But what always worked for him, or so he thought, was his power to control his chosen victims through his mind bending and hypnotic skills; he desperately tried to permeate Flora's thoughts but she was one step ahead. Her meditation skills had taught her strength of mind and could easily rise above the spell which Orbotron was trying so desperately to cast upon her.

She plunged into the woods, armed with a plan, knowing the alien would follow her. And, so he did. This young lady was taking a huge risk by going alone. Black Sun and Black Knight were the only remaining Vams who were still at large, as were a couple of Ratscorps who had escaped Atohi's wrath. So, she had to be careful. She felt no fear as her faithful bird of paradise Sky swooped down to her side. Flora knew this land like no other, she knew where she was heading and her plan was to lure Orbotron into his death trap. This would take place in the ancient waters at the Fountain of Pure Senses.

The Fountain of Pure Senses has been around since time began According to the Legend, the Fountain is a font of knowledge, wisdom and has amazing healing properties in its waters. Just one droplet of this precious water has the power to cure a multitude of ailments.

Towards beings who show no threat, the fountain is most welcoming and embraces whoever or whatever cares to enter, but if any sign of evil enters the waters, their presence is immediately detected and the soothing, healing powers cease for that time. Then the fountain takes on a different role; its crystal clearness, at first, appears harmless enough but then the water is fiercely projected into an uncontrollable torrent of acidic, bubbling streams enslaving and trapping its evil victim. These flows are so powerful it can drag its victim deep under into a ferocious, gushing, gurgling whirlpool, a vortex which leads deep underneath the very bowels of the earth, from which there is no escape. The evil is trapped, and the Fountain of Pure Senses is magically restored back to its usual harmonious state.

This dramatic fate was now long time due to the ego possessed alien, Orbotron. He had no idea of the forthcoming events but Flora was about to make sure it was coming to him fast.

Flora proceeded with great speed through the heavily wooded groves, the fireflies once again showed their presence and helped to illuminate the paths until every inch of the dense woodland grove was lit by a tiny firefly. Flora could not help but admire them; every light was a sign of hope and victory as it spurred her on faster and faster through the undergrowth, she proceeded forthwith.

Orbotron with his gift of levitation was closing in on her fast. He was so close that, at times, she could hear his deep breathing. But Flora took comfort in the thought that every passing second was leading him closer to his fate, so she just had to keep moving and let the alien follow her.

Flora had calculated her moves precisely, she was now in close proximity of the fountain and would soon reach her destination. The closer she got, the unmistakable sounds of running water became clearer and clearer. She could even smell the freshness and feel the energising droplets sprayed by the fountain in the atmosphere. And then, through the deep emerald of the grove, she caught the first sight of the spectacular vision which was the Fountain of Pure Senses, flowing out of a great Marble rock.

Fortunately, the alien's toxic mix had not reached this sacred glade. The sun still shone here. Unbeknown to strangers, the fountain was protected at all times by an unforeseen membrane so no damage could ever be bestowed upon it. This Fountain was sacred to the whole island, it was also an ancient font, which could protect our world too.

On entering the glade, like sweet music, the waters called out to Flora immediately, "Come, come, my child. Take my waters, let me heal you, let me banish the evil who follows you from worlds beyond," with no time to loose, Flora took heed and flung herself into the fountain. She had literally seconds to absorb the positive vibes which engulfed every inch of her body, the waters called out to her again, "Flora, Flora, beware," as she turned round. Just then Orbotron had entered the glade, he was about to jump in too but with haste, Flora clambered out of the fountain, and carefully crossed to the other side. She took cover under the shelter of the marble rock formation and waited with baited breath.

Under the protection of the rock, she did not have to wait long to witness the drastic transformation which was enfolding right in front of her. As soon as Orbotron immersed himself into the fountain, his fate was truly sealed. The ferocious whirlpool whipped him up into a gurgling, putrid yellow froth, sucking him further and further into the water. The speed of that whirlpool was just unbelievable; nothing could stand a chance within its flow.

From her hiding place, Flora could just make out the aliens spindly long fingers clutching at the air. He must be waiting on his mutants to come and rescue him but no one would come. It was too late for him now.

Orbotron, the master of planet Mutraculon, creator of mutant populations and toxic gases had met his doom in the gigantic swirl of this powerful fountain, his lifeless body with cape still intact, had been dragged and swallowed by the vortex which lead to the Caverns of Eternity, buried in the deepest bowels of the earth. And so, with that the Fountain of Pure Senses had fulfilled its purpose once again. This time it had rid the island and our world of a mega force which had been at large for just too long!

Flora for some time remained speechless as she clung to that marble rock for dear life. She had felt the power of the waters, as the earth had shook violently beneath her. Sky, the bird of paradise, landed down by her side. He had been watching her all the while and had come to guide her back to the Path of Palms. Flora was more than grateful for the company. She turned and look towards the graceful bird, with the look of victory written all over her beautiful face, "Our island is safe, and now planet earth can start again. The end of Orbotron would ignite and signal an immediate healing process."

"Oh! Fountain of Pure Senses our Saviour," cried out Flora with an elated tone, "How can I ever thank you? Our island and the human world will be eternally grateful for your bravest of deeds."

"Flora, my dear," answered the waters, "that was my job, I was created by forces of Nature and kingdoms beyond to heal and replenish and that is what I have done today."

"Go back now, sweet girl, back to your Path of Palms, to announce the good news!!!"

"Tonight, you must celebrate the downfall of Orbotron. Tonight, the whole Island will rejoice in the glory. But remember this, dear child. When you need me, I will be here in my glade as I have always been."

Flora promised that she would return to the glade, and then she swiftly left with the bird of paradise in close proximity. They meandered through the deep grove, the toxic mist was no more, and a clear path through the emerald glades was set before them. Flora could feel the spongy ferns and the deep roots of the ancient trees and the tingling sensation made her feel alive and revived all her senses as did the woody earthy smells that lingered in the air and filled her lungs with sweet, sweet oxygen.

glades, I was heading towards the Fountain of Pure Senses in the marble rocks on the other side of the island. Now try to imagine the fountain as kind of like a large Jacuzzi, but not just a normal relaxing Jacuzzi like you people have back at home but a Jacuzzi gone crazy, out of control like a mini tsunami, if you like. With me so far???"

Still slightly confused, but eager to find out what Flora was hoping to tell them, they encouraged her to carry on.

"Well, the unsuspecting Orbotron was sucked into its centre vortex and was spun around and around at speeds that were just off the scale. The vortex is the entrance to a chamber that leads its victims into the Caverns of Eternity, and that my friends, is where Orbotron met his doom!"

"Wow!!! What an ending," exclaimed Eddie Eezzie who was just about getting his head around all this.

"So there you have it, guys."

"Now I have a question for all of you, the mutants? What has become of the mutants? Are there any survivors?"

It was Atohi who stepped forward to explain, "Unfortunately, we believe two large Vamcreepers managed to flee, and possibly a couple of Ratscorps may have survived. We believe the Vams have fled upwards towards the mountain range in the east of the island. But on a positive note, it is highly unlikely that they will survive. With Orbotron gone, and the purest of pure atmosphere here on the island, this alone will certainly cause some complications for our mutant friends."

"I agree," commented Flora. "Thank you, Atohi, thank you all, the spirit of the island is safe, and you should all be very proud of yourselves."

"And that calls for a celebration!!!"

And celebrate, they did!!! The celebrations continued long into the night. Eddie and his band members, who had now returned to normal after the death of Orbotron, were on top form. Obviously, it was none other than them who provided the entertainment for the evening, and it must be said, it all went down in Raw Rocking Style. Whoever was out at sea that night, surely would have heard them as the whole island rocked with their sounds!!!!!

Meanwhile, young readers, sorry to interrupt the happy flow of things but I must explain to you what became of the three mutants still at large on the Island of Sacred Souls.

Chapter 35

As we all know by now that Orbotron is no more but there is one thing that may leave us a little bit uncertain.

Orbotron created his flock of hellish birds by crossing a black crow with a vampire bat; he added growth hormones to create a much larger more threatening creature. He also implanted a microscopic chip in the skulls of the birds which was complete with a tracking device. Orbotron, as we know, was a controlling character and he was very proud of his microscopic tracking devices.

His first Vamcreeper, Black Sun, hatched after six weeks in an incubator, which was kept in a laboratory within the vaults of the Silver Oval. This little chick was soon to grow into the most feared Vamcreeper ever to darken the skies.

The alien had often thought that the hatching of the chick was one of his proudest moments. With these Vamcreepers on board, he would prove to be unstoppable in his plans. He was thrilled with Black Sun and proceeded to feed and care for him; nourishing his ever-growing appetite with small birds, frogs, lizards, insects, and as you can imagine the chick flourished and grew super strong.

When the Vamp was ready to leave the security of the incubator, Orbotron even taught him how to fly by taking him into his glass atrium with its tall and wide ceilings mirroring the sky outside, he would let the Vamcreeper fly free within this great hall of glass and the huge creature took naturally and immediately to flight.

From this one super mutant, Orbotron would clone the rest of his flock, next to hatch successfully was Black Knight. Out of a batch of some 10,000 eggs and so it is that Black Knight and Black Sun. The only remaining Vamcreepers are out there somewhere after fleeing to the mountains in the east of the island.

They have settled inside the ancient walls of a barren cave, you could say, an ideal setting for a bat like creature, as here it is always dark and gloomy and they continued to survive. There is also some kind of safety capsule within the microchip which forced their bodies into a state of suspended animation. There, they hang upside down just like bats until the day of awakening.

As for the only remaining Ratscorp, she made it down to the bottom of the spiral rock formation and took cover deep underground; tucked away in a burrow, the mutant has settled down for a very long sleep indeed.

Part 3

Chapter 36

The Return Back Home
Regrowth of the Planet
The City of Hanley

21st May 2051

Flora's Teachings

Aranck decided to stay with Flora on the Island of Sacred Souls. Atohi and the Good Tribes People were more than happy to let him stay, as both Aranck and Flora made an amazing knowledgeable couple and had so much to learn from each other. Their precious collaboration would seal their fates with pride, enabling them to become the greatest of Guardians for the Island and Planet Earth.

As for JG and the others, the last few months spent on the island were of peace and tranquillity. Flora was an amazing teacher and JG learned that her enthusiasm for her work was second to none. She taught JG everything she knew from plants, animals and aquatic life; ranging from their daily care, to preservation, conservation, and the co-ordination of breeding projects for every life form which included endangered species. With this acquired precious knowledge, JG could not wait to return home and put Flora's teachings into practice.

JG could only but feel proud to be within the presence of this wonderful girl, he often wondered where her parents and family were but did not like to pry.

Before JG's imminent departure, and on the last day of his Island adventure, Flora asked him, Gabriel and Aranck to follow her down to the beach. She explained to them she had recently been caring for two orphaned dolphin pups and today would be the day to release them back into the wild. She had asked JG to be present at this such occasion so he could witness this wonderful experience first-hand, to keep it as an everlasting memory in the name of conservation.

As the group neared the lagoon, where Flora had been caring for the dolphins, the two pups immediately swam over to greet their guests.

"Wow!!!" exclaimed JG. "They are so friendly," he could not wait to enter the water so he could get even closer to the friendly pair. Aranck could not resist either, so the two young men waded in followed closely by Flora. The dolphins immediately responded and welcomed the group, as they invited them to swim with them, chattering with delight they nudged the boys with their noses and spun around and around, diving and bounding, in and out of the lagoon.

JG had never experienced such close proximity to a wild dolphin, they truly were amazing animals. He looked into their large expressive eyes, and felt a form of mutual understanding flowing between him and the dolphin pair.

"They are reading you," said Flora. "These beings are highly intelligent."

JG was bowled over by the experience, "Extraordinary," replied JG, as he rubbed their smooth noses; they flipped over onto their backs for a quick tummy rub.

Flora would miss this cheeky pair, but knew it was time for them to go back into the wilds to live a full life as nature intended in that vast ocean. Who knows, they may come back to visit her one day, she thought. So with tears in her big soft brown eyes, she bent down and kissed both the dolphins on their noses and said, "OK you two, time for your big moment, back into the wild."

"JG, Aranck, I could use the help of some strong muscle bound young men to move that boulder over here, this will enable the dolphins to swim out to sea."

"OK, your wish is my command," joked back Aranck. "Coming up!!!!! Whatever you say," he smiled a cheeky smile, which lit up Flora's face. She thought how lucky she was to have this great guy around permanently, to help her and keep her company.

Finally with much shoving and pushing and shear brute strength exercised by both young men, the boulder finally came free and a clear channel out to sea was provided for the dolphins. They sensed the opening immediately, and at first, they were slightly hesitant to leave Flora and the safety of the lagoon but they took one giant leap of faith, they smiled looking around at the last group for the last time. Their expressive eyes lighting up their faces and then off they swam dipping and diving through the bouncy waves.

Flora and the others huddled together on the beach proudly watching the dolphins, as they bounded with ease further and further into the open sea.

"A perfect ending to a perfect experience," announced JG, as he wiped a single tear away from his eyes. He blushed slightly on noticing this but nobody commented. "The dolphins' return to the wild really does sum everything up Flora," JG continued, "I understand now why you wanted me to take part in their release to freedom."

"I knew you would JG, and that was your last lesson from me," (for a while anyway) Flora smiled encouragingly, "and I would like to add that I can proudly say that you have successfully graduated into a full-fledged Ecologist with hands on experience. Well Done!!!!! Take a bow, my friend," they had all been through so much together and were all extremely proud of JG. Now he had to make the next step of the journey alone, although, not quite alone as Gabriel and Jericho would be with him every inch of the way. The teachings of both Flora and Aranck were now firmly sealed into his soul.

That last night spent on the island, before drifting off to sleep, JG had thoughts of Flora. Like I mentioned before, he had often wondered where her parents were, she had never spoken of them or of any relatives for that matter. For this reason, he was more than thrilled that Aranck and chosen to stay with her.

As he continued with his thoughts, something told him to look inside the manuscript. Yes, the very manuscript that had been so special to this very journey, the very manuscript that had brought them here to this island; I suppose, the very same manuscript had started all of this in the first place, when JG had taken it out of the City Library, back home in Hanley.

He was drawn to a verse titled the Fountain of Pure Senses, and it narrates like this:

Some will say she was born and first appeared from the fountain of pure senses. Like the fountain, flora is ageless, a timeless beauty to remain forever young; a true spirit of nature and a chosen guardian.

Blessed to tend and protect the island of sacred souls, and to guide mother earth through the passage of time.

He smiled, closed the book and decided to leave it here with Flora. He imagined that this is where the book had first been written, it had come full circle and had been rightfully brought back to where it belonged. On Flora's bookcase, there was even a space for it, and yes, you guessed it, the ancient manuscript just fitted in perfectly.

Chapter 37

The Return Home

City of Hanley – the Park on the Hill

It was Atohi's words that first awoke JG.

"Wake up, wake up, JG," Atohi spoke calmly and encouragingly. "You are home, you are back in Hanley, remember these words," Atohi continued, "I am here for you, whenever you need me."

JG finally opened his eyes to feel the warmth of the sun on his face. He did not know for how long he had been asleep and undoubtedly felt a little hazy. It was comforting to know that his faithful friends Gabriel and Jericho lay close by his side. He glanced upwards into the deep blue sky, and immediately responded to the familiar surroundings, city sounds, city smells, "No it can't be, you mean to tell me," he jumped up, rather surprised. "We are back home, we are back in Hanley!"

"Yes, that is so true," Gabriel responded, "and if I may add, I think things are going to get a little bit better from now on. On first appearances, it seems that the pollution levels of previous times had subsided considerably, there is a new freshness in the air, it actually feels that the veil has been lifted and new life is springing up everywhere you look."

"All sounds good!" replied JG, rising shakily to his feet. "Wow!!!!! Weeee!!! This sensation is strange, it is like I have been out for days, I recall no journey back here, and the boat where is the boat?????"

"Don't worry JG, Atohi, as usual, has taken care of everything for us. I promise you, when you return back home later today, everything will be just as you left it and the boat, well, she will be back in her boathouse as if she has never even set sail."

"As for your mum, dad and your friends, they will be none the wiser to them it is like you have been here all the time. Nothing has changed in their minds, time has kind of stood still, while we crossed worlds and bent time all in the name of conservation and preservation of the planet."

"When you think of it that way, Wow!!! We are real heroes," said JG.

"Something like that," winked Gabriel.

"Come on then, we can't sit here all day. We have work to do," perked up Jericho, "you two boys, hey!"

The three set off across the park in high spirits, it was spring and everything seemed right with the world; flocks of birds had started to breed again. Sparrows, robins, finches and other species chirped in and out of the trees and bathed in the warm spring sunshine. Insects were also in abundance; butterflies, bees, dragonflies and the like added to the spring scene. The beauty of it all was unfolding before their eyes, plants and flowers were in full bud in this park. At least Orbotron's mark had been clearly wiped off the slate, and it was an encouraging sign, just practically days after his death.

Obviously, Hanley would remain a modern city and the buildings of concrete and steel would continue to dominate the landscape, but JG realised a vital point, a balance could be achieved between nature and the modern world.

JG instinctively knew what he had to do and how to put Aranck's and Flora's teachings into practice, he looked upon it as his duty to educate his generation and children of a younger age. He had some great ideas buzzing around in that young head of his, of course, he would need help from his friends and their cool musical talents and dance skills. And maybe, if they had any time, some input from Galaxy's End which would be most welcome. They were a sure bet on how to motivate people, those guys could really reach the masses.

With all this swimming around in his head, JG was more than determined to commence his quest. He would head back home now, but first he had an inkling, he just wanted to take a quick detour. "Gabes, Jeri are you with me? There is something I just want to check out."

"JG, where are you going?" cried out Gabriel, "Like I said you two, just a quick detour, it won't take long." Gabriel and

Jericho followed reluctantly, and actually they were a little curious, and wanted to find out what JG had in mind.

They did not have to wait long, they soon realised where they were heading; the Financial Quarter. JG needed to know how things were at the Silver Oval, the late Orbotron's domain.

Bustling traffic, busy people, nonstop action, a stark contrast to the peaceful island from where they had recently returned from.

They turned into the main square of the financial district and quite literally stopped in their tracks, mouths aghast wide open. The Silver Oval was no more, it was completely eradicated. All that remained was a gigantic pile of rubble, a multi-million pound building just gone, just like that.

"But how? And when did this happen?" JG exclaimed out loud, a smartly dressed businessman standing nearby was more than happy to explain, and he went on to say—

"As you may probably be aware, the Silver Oval always held such mystery and nobody ever knew who the owner was. My bank dealt with a huge sum of money, I am talking huge from a mystery client."

"When the project was first approved some 10 years ago, no meetings were ever held, and the bank staff and managers never got to know who this extremely rich business man was. Every transaction was done over the internet. Communications between the two parties were done by either letter or email, nobody even spoke to this person."

"Although no questions were asked, whoever they were, the one sure thing we did know about them was that they were filthy stinking rich, and banks being banks were more than happy to take on this investment and co-ordinate every deal for their mystery client."

"Then about a week ago, early one Friday evening, strange sounds could be heard. Deep rumblings were being reported by people coming from the direction of the Silver Oval, a large crack had appeared, which began to cause quite a panic, and then a mist came down, which literally covered the whole building. The rumblings grew stronger and the surrounding areas started to shake like an earthquake. The tremors were reported some ten miles away from the other side of the city."

"Then all of a sudden, there was a loud crash! A bolt of thunder and flashes of lighting appeared in the murky sky above, the building collapsed glass littered the streets below, people were running for their lives avoiding the heavy shards at all costs."

"With haste, emergency teams were called in and the area was evacuated. Luckily, there were no casualties but the next morning all that remained was this mammoth sized pile of decimated silver rocks."

"What an interesting story," said JG. "Thank you, sir. You have been most informative," he said to the young businessman.

"Have you any idea what will happen to the land now and this huge square?" requested JG.

"Yes, I think the banks and the City Mayor, in the not too distant future, will be expecting some propositions in the form of tenders to bid for this amazing space. There are already a lot of extremely wealthy business people interested in this most notorious area."

"Why have you any ideas, young man?" The smart businessman winked at JG, and handed him a business card.

"I think I might, I just might have a wonderful idea!!!!! And this huge space would be more than ideal for my plans."

"Good. I like to see fresh ideas coming from the youth, I wish you all the luck in the world. You seem like a very intelligent young man indeed." The young businessman winked once again.

"Thanks for everything, and it has been great chatting with you, most informative," JG said, and without even looking at the card, he placed it carefully into his inside pocket.

"Remember to call me, I will do all that is within my power to help you realise your dream," he winked once again, a wink of familiarity, which touched JG deeply and sincerely, and with that the young man disappeared into the bustling crowd.

Chapter 38

With more enthusiasm than ever, his plans with each passing moment were becoming even more realistic. The three started to make their way out of the city and towards the suburbs. In less than an hour JG would be back home again, his parents would be there to greet him. When he finally turned into his road, he could no longer keep the huge smile off his face. A feeling of comfort and great warmth filled his heart, JG and the two dogs bounded up the garden path and then in his usual way he somersaulted across the front lawn.

"Mum, Dad, where are you both?" he cried out excitedly, it was a perfect Spring Day and both his parents were outside in the back garden. On hearing JG cry out, his parents both looked up. "Son, calm down. Why so hysterical?" Mum asked.

"Oh!!! Because it is lunchtime, of course!!!!!" said Dad. "Our growing son has returned home hungry."

"Oh, now I get it," said Mum. "Yes, they always return home when they need feeding," she joked on.

"Phew!!!!! Phew!!!!! And double phew!!!!!" it was completely like he had been told, time had stood still. Atohi had been true to his word. His parents were none the wiser.

No long explanations, no harm done, wonderful, JG thought, slumping back into his favourite deckchair, basking under the warm spring sun. He reached for the card in his pocket eagerly and began to read the bold inscription, staring at the wording it read as follows—

Aaron Oakley – Junior Business Advisor
The Royal Hanley Bank Corporation
Aka – Aranck – The Land That Once Was – The Whispering Planes

For a moment, JG could not believe it, it had been Aranck all along. That crafty fellow had crossed time again and switched worlds just like that, "How does he do it?????" JG was in complete awe of him.

"Ah, so that is why that businessman seemed so familiar, well, that's Aranck for you, just letting me know that he is not that far away. He is the master of shape shifting and has definitely taken the art to another level with his expertise. He can cross dimensions and places in time."

JG was desperate to learn this higher level in the art. Gabriel had assured him, all in good time, but that would be another story, meaning, another life changing adventure to the Land that Once Was, and the Whispering Planes.

For now, he had enough to deal with. He could only be glad that his dear friend had his back and was even willing to pose as a Junior Bank Advisor in order to help him.

That evening JG retired to bed early. He wanted to be ready and fresh for tomorrow as soon as his head hit the pillow, he sunk into a deep and energising sleep.

The following morning JG had some explaining to do. Dad had discovered Gabriel sleeping in the boat shed in early hours. He had awoken early and had gone in to do his usual maintenance work on the boat. He had discovered the handsome Wolf Dog there, sleeping soundly on the top deck. To say Dad was shocked was an understatement. At first sight, Gabriel could be confused for a wild wolf, he did not want to stick around long enough to find out. He rushed back into the house leaving the sleeping Gabriel peacefully on the boat.

"JG, son, are you awake? You have some explaining to do. Guess what I discovered in the boat shed? Yes, a Wolf Dog, does he have anything to do with you?"

"Well, Dad, to be perfectly honest, yes he does. His name is Gabriel, and he is just wonderful. He is special, you know. The poor thing has been sleeping on the streets abandoned from a very young age. He really needs a good home, Dad. And Jeri, well Jeri she just loves him." JG was so eager to impress his dad and was desperately trying to convince him to let Gabriel stay.

Dad being Dad was a bit of a soft touch really, and especially where dogs were concerned, you could say, Dad saw the wonderful wild spirit that Gabriel projected to the outside world from within. He was quietly impressed by the Wolf Dog. And to JG's joy, agreed to let Gabriel stay.

"Jericho, did you hear that girl? Gabes is staying. Oh, Dad, you are the best! You won't regret this. Gabriel finally has found a forever loving family home."

With so many good things going on right now, JG thought that to keep the momentum going. It was a good time to round up all his friends and tell them about his plans for the Financial Quarter. So what was next on the agenda? Off to Ricky's house. Yes, that was the place where dreams were created in none other than Ricky's attic bedroom.

Flying through the door, JG mounted his BMX and within seconds he was en-route to Ricky the Red's.

Pulling up outside Ricky's front door, JG enthusiastically called out his friend's name, "Ricky my man, are you at home?" Then in response Ricky cried out in his usual manner, "Who goes there? Be it a mate or foe, I need to know. Yo! Yo! Yo! Yo! Yo!" Dudes, his crazy red curls were what you first saw as he stuck his head out of the attic bedroom window.

Once settled inside, the two bet mates got down to a real serious chat. Ricky was crazy and joked around but if you really needed him to be serious and intelligent, he could be that too. In fact, he was a really good listener and was intrigued by what JG had to say.

Although he knew nothing of JG's secret escapades, the island and other world adventures, what JG was explaining was of real interest to Ricky, and he was determined to help his friend.

The theme of the discussion was focused around JG's ecological quest, and balancing nature with the new, fast present modern world.

First thing discussed on the agenda was putting together an interactive online youth project based on Flora's teachings. This would educate the young generation about the importance of conservation and encouraging it into our daily lives, ultimately, achieving a balance of harmony and co-existence with the planet.

Next they discussed, now this is where Ricky knew his stuff: Music Events. What the guys were planning would be an organisation of regular music and dance events. Possibly on a monthly basis, organised by the youth for the youth with all proceeds going to yes, you have guessed it, saving the planet.

So, this was JG's proposition, which hopefully, would soon be ready to present to the Mayor of the City and the Bank of Hanley: To create A National Park in the bustling Financial Quarter, (where the Silver Oval once stood dominating the landscape) for all to use and enjoy JG's Master Plan:

Hanley's Haven of Hope

An island oasis in the centre of the vast metropolis which would include an Educational centre/conservation and zoological park, acres of natural beauty, where new trees would be planted for all to enjoy and admire, meadows and water features including a lake for family day trippers to visit and live the beauty of the great outdoors.

A rehoming service for abandoned animals in name of Gabriel, being the proud patron of this service would also be commissioned, and finally a state of the art Studio for Music, Arts, Theatre and Dance Projects, a place young people could be proud of and make it their very own.

Quick as a whiz, the two friends had the whole project designed and professionally ready to tender high hopes were set. They were going to approach the Mayor and the Bank of Hanley tomorrow. JG at this point was relieved to know that Aaron Oakley (Junior Financial Advisor) aka Aranck would be at hand to offer any help they needed. JG was banking on him (pardon the pun) to clench the deal for them.

"Now, there is just one thing," said Ricky, the Red, as the two friends glanced proudly at their work. He proceeded, "JG you and I have been best mates since the first day at primary school. I know that you have always cared about animals and the good of the planet, but I am astonished at how much profound knowledge you have on the subject. It is as if you have studied for a master's in ecology or something. If I didn't know any better, I would call you a genius. You amaze me!"

"Well, you know," answered JG. "Sometimes in life, you find yourself in situations, and in some way, I feel that I have attracted certain forces from different places. It is as if they chose me, if you like."

“But who? What? JG, you are not making any sense with this. Now I am intrigued,” continued Ricky. “Tell me! Tell me!” he pleaded. “If it needs to be kept a secret, your secret will be safe with me.” Ricky needed the full story, he was not one to be happy with short answers.

“Put it this way Ricky, my mate, between you and I, let us just say I have been on a journey, and consequently have been inspired and have learnt so much through these new experiences. Things that you would never have thought possible, things that are not of this world, ancient traditions and beliefs that apply completely to the way we must care for our planet. Since the beginning of time, this knowledge has been gifted for all to share, you just need to look deeper and see things in a slightly different way.”

JG winked at his friend. Ricky still was not happy with JG’s answer and pushed again for another response.

“Come on, JG,” said Ricky. “Where exactly have you been? And who or what exactly did you meet?”

JG winked at his friend again, “Now that would be telling, would it not? All in good time, my mate. All in good time, you just have to be patient and keep trusting me on this.”

“I will get it out of you one way or another,” Ricky announced stubbornly but with a broad smile across his face, as he reached for one of his guitars.

“Come on, mate. Let us get this wrapped up, we have a mayor and a bank to impress!” JG exclaimed.

“The future of nature’s message is in our hands Hanley’s Haven.”

The Hands of the Youth.

Chapter 34

Flora could only hope that her beloved Path of Palms had returned to its normal state, and that all her friends and animal companions were safe and hopefully, waiting for her return.

JG and Aranck were the first to notice the approaching Flora, as she bounded with pure elation and outstretched arms into her clearing. Smiles all around for this happy group, you could say the feeling was more than mutual, the Path of Palms once again lavished itself under the golden sunshine, as the soft sand warmed by the sun cushioned the soles of their feet. The exotic smells from the abundance of plants and flowers, helped to build the perfect atmosphere for which this island was famous for.

You could say just for a time, the whole group was lost in the moment. A universal calm had been bestowed upon them, as gratitude and hope filled the mood.

Presently it was Flora who broke the silence. “Well guys, I think we can say victory is ours!!!!! Orbotron is no more.”

“Really, really!” exclaimed JG. “He is dead! You mean that fiend is really dead?”

“Yes, JG, The Fountain of Pure Senses, shall we say kindly disposed of him for us, and he got his just deserts. Let us just say, he came to a real swash-bucking, wash-buckling whirlpool end!!!!!”

“Excuse me!!! Can you repeat that! That bit about the swash and wash end?” JG was quite confused.

Flora certainly knew how to build and keep them all in suspense, she knew these guys were always interested in a bit of an adventure, and it was good to keep them guessing, the party mood was already in full flow, she thought.

“OK, gather around my friends and I will begin,” she proceeded to narrate the end of Orbotron. “OK, let’s look at it like this. Orbotron, as I had planned followed me through the